LOVING HARD

Eight Second Ride Book 2

I0520215

Sandy Sullivan

Erotic Romance

Erotic Romance

Falling Hard
Copyright © 2015 Sandy Sullivan
E-book ISBN: 978-1-944122-19-5

First E-book Publication: December 2015

Cover design by Dawné Dominique
Edited by Stephanie Balistreri
Proofread by Ariana Gaynor
All cover art and logo copyright © 2015 by Sandy Sullivan

Dedication

This is dedicated to the fans of two men falling in love as well as hot cowboy bull riders. Being a fan of cowboys, I couldn't wait to see how having two of them together would be. I think they are hotter than hot and I hope you agree.

LOVING HARD
Eight Second Ride Book 2

Sandy Sullivan

Chapter One

Excruciating pain shot from his hip to his toes. God, he hurt. Rusty Arnold moaned softly as he adjusted his leg. Damn bad luck. He'd been on top, number one in the world standings and with nothing more than a twist of fate, he'd been knocked out for the season with a snapped femur.

After his ninety point ride ended his run for the championship, his father had shown up to bring him home. Laid out in the back of his dad's pickup, the trip back to New Mexico hadn't been pleasant. It had been smooth in some spots but once they got to the home place, the driveway bumps killed his leg. Pain pills didn't touch the ache from the drive. *This driveway needs to be graveled again. These potholes are going to kill me.*

As they drove up to the house and the truck came to a stop, he sighed with relief. Now to figure out how to get into the house without hurting himself, would be the trick of the century. He had crutches, but maneuvering on those on a gravel walkway wouldn't be fun. He couldn't count on his brothers to help either. Most of them were probably out riding fences or herding cattle this time of day.

"Rusty?"

"Yeah?"

"You all right?"

"No, Dad. My leg hurts like hell and I have to figure out how to get into the house." Rusty scooted from the top of the bed of the truck to where his leg reached the tailgate. The hard cast from his groin to his ankle would be interesting to get out without beaning him somewhere he didn't need to get hit.

With his jeans cut from hip to hem flapping in the late summer breeze, sweat formed on his lip from the exertion of trying to move. Stabbing pain hit him full force. He tried to breathe through it so he could figure out how to move without the further agony.

"You can brace yourself on me and use one crutch. Your mother will grab the other one. She's made up the bedroom downstairs for you since you won't be able to make the stairs with that cast."

"Thanks. I appreciate it. Are the others out?"

"This time of day? Of course they are. It takes a team to run this place, Rusty, not that you've been around here for the last several years."

Great. Lecture time. "I've been kind of busy, Dad, taking care of my own place."

"Chasin' the bull ridin' circuit."

"That too. It's what I've chosen to do. I'm sorry if you don't understand."

"As the eldest, your place is here on the home place, not gallivanting all over the damn country trying to get yourself killed." He jammed his hands on his hips. "Now look at you, busted up, and home with your tail between your legs."

"I'm a grown man, Dad. I need to take care of my own. You have Russell here to help run this place. I'm good with my own and plus, I'll be back by the beginning of next season."

"Figures." His father stepped forward. "Well, come on then. Let's get you in the house. Your momma will bring you some water so you can take more pills if you need them."

He groaned as he slowly lowered the casted leg toward the ground and blood rushed to his toes. He'd had the leg propped up in the back of the pickup during the ride to help reduce the swelling, but now that it was down, it began to throb in earnest. "Fuck."

"Watch your mouth."

"Sorry. It really friggin' hurts."

"I imagine."

His father jammed his shoulder under Rusty's armpit, hoisting him into a semi-standing position as his mother rushed down the steps.

"Rusty, honey, let me help."

Dots swam before his eyes. He shook his head to clear it, but that didn't help much. Nausea cramped his stomach. He probably shouldn't have taken the last set of pills on an empty stomach. "Just get the crutch, Mom, and help me put it under my arm." He blew out a breath trying to work through the nausea so he didn't puke right there in the front yard.

"Okay?"

"Yeah."

With his arm around his father's shoulders, he hobbled to the front of the porch. They managed to help him get up the two steps with the crutch and his father's strength, so he could work his way into the house, down the short hallway, and into the downstairs bedroom.

He collapsed on the bed the moment he got close enough to the mattress. His mother hovered over him.

"What can I do, Rusty?"

"Nothing at the moment, Ma. I need to rest a second, and then I'll be able to get my leg up on the bed."

"But I can help." She bent down and started to lift his casted leg.

"No!"

She dropped it back on the floor, banging his heel on the hardwood. "Fuck."

His mother stood with her hands on her hips in what he liked to call the *disgusted mother* look. "Rusty, enough with the language."

"Sorry, but that hurt!"

"I understand, but I was only trying to help."

He fell back on the bed, staring at the ceiling while his leg throbbed with every beat of his heart. His thigh ached as he rubbed the cast, hoping beyond hope it would help. Of course, it didn't. He needed something to drink, preferably a shot of whiskey even though he knew that wouldn't do, and a heavy duty pain pill. "I know, but really, it's better if I do it myself."

"All right then." She wiped her hands on the full apron she wore around the front of her body. He couldn't remember a time she hadn't worn an apron. "I will get some food started. It's almost lunch time."

The pain began to subside a little as he maneuvered his leg up onto the bed and leaned his back against the headboard. "Can you turn on the television? I want to watch to see who will win this week and the final round is on."

"Really, Rusty? It's not enough for you to want to break your neck riding bulls, but you have to watch it too?"

"These are my friends, Ma. It's important to me to see who wins. There's one guy who's making really good rides right now, and I'm hoping he continues so he can get into the finals in a few months."

"I think all of you are crazy in the head."

"I know."

She flipped on the old, small television sitting on the dresser. It was circa 1980, but at least it was television. His parents opted for cable, thank goodness. "What channel, Rusty?"

"It's on CBS."

She turned on the network station on the television. The screen glowed with the colors of the bull riding circuit. The dirt, the clang of the metal gates, the roar of the crowd, everything got his heart racing. He sat up higher in the bed, squinting to bring the screen in focus better. "Ma, can you grab my glasses from my gear bag? I don't have my contacts in. They made me take them out at the hospital." After she rummaged around in his bag for a moment, she produced the gold wire-rimmed glasses. He took them from her hand, placing them on his nose and the ear pieces around his ears. "Thanks."

"All set now so I can get lunch started?"

"I need the pills that are in there too and a glass of water, please. My leg is killing me with all this moving around."

"How long will you be in the cast?"

"Six to eight weeks or more. It depends on how it's healing. I have an appointment with the doctor in two weeks to check it. They aren't sure whether I will need surgery or not."

She handed him the pill bottle. "It's a good thing we live close to Albuquerque so you can get proper care."

"Yeah."

"I'll be right back with some water."

"Thanks, Ma. I love you."

"I love you too, Rusty." She leaned in a kissed him on the forehead. "Your brothers will be glad you're home. You know Thomas and Junior idolize you."

"I know. I'll be glad to see them too."

"Well then." She smoothed her apron down the front of her dress before she walked out of the room, leaving him to watch the action on the television.

Levi Bond was up next. He hoped Levi did well. He was a friend as friends went on the circuit, but Rusty thought Levi had a good shot at the finals if he kept riding bulls.

Rusty sat up, staring intently at the screen. Levi did his wrap and leaned into the shoulders of the bull, before nodding for the gate. Rusty held his breath. This was the same bull Levi had been riding the week before when he dislocated his shoulder. This animal was one of the best athletes on the circuit and one of the toughest bulls to ride. Levi almost made it look easy although Rusty knew it was anything but. Rusty sighed as the buzzer sounded. It was a decent ride, nothing spectacular, but he held on for eight which meant he got a score. When the announcer relayed the total, Rusty pumped his fist in the air just as the television showed Levi doing the same. "Yes!"

There were several guys on the circuit he was friends with, but he held Levi in the highest regard. See, Levi was gay. He didn't flaunt it around everyone, but most of the guys knew he was. Rusty counted Levi as one of his close knit group. It didn't bother Rusty that Levi preferred men. Some of the guys didn't like it though.

Rusty adjusted his leg for a little more comfort as his mother returned with the bottle of water. "Thanks, Mom."

"You're welcome, sweetie. I'll be back in a bit with your lunch. The rest of the group should be returning soon, so I'm sure your brothers will be coming in to say hello."

"Maybe."

"They love you, Rusty, even if they are a little bit mad that you aren't here to help in between working your place and riding bulls."

"I know, but they have to understand, this is what I want to do."

"They do."

"I don't think so."

"Well, Russell and John don't really understand, and then there are the hands we still have on the place who believe you should be here helping rather than running all over the countryside, but overall, it's okay."

"Dad doesn't understand."

"No, he doesn't really. He believes you should give up this nonsense and come home."

"It's in the blood, Ma. I can't explain it. Plus, I still have my place to run, so I wouldn't be here much anyway."

She pressed her palm to his cheek. "I know, honey. Men must do what they must do."

"Do you ever wish you had a girl?"

"Sometimes when I'm cooking and I wish I had someone to teach all the household chores to, someone to go shopping with or someone to look forward to a pretty wedding for, but I love you boys with all of my heart, and I wouldn't trade you for the world." She dabbed at the corner of her eye with her apron. "Now, take your pills, and I'll bring lunch when it's finished." She softly closed the door behind her.

He focused back on the screen. Two more riders had gone and been bucked off. His stomach clenched each time the rider gave the nod. It was like he was the one in the chute, but no, he was hold up here on the family place with his leg in a cast for the next several weeks. He would probably go out of his mind before all was said and done. He wanted to be there with the dirt swirling, the roaring of the crowd, and the camaraderie of his fellow riders. Most of all, he would miss the one guy he'd had his eye on for a long time.

No way could he reveal to his family his preferences. They would never understand. If he didn't bring home a woman for his mother to love, his father to dote on, and his brothers to admire, he would be cast out of the family like yesterday's trash. His family didn't understand his need to ride bulls, they would never understand his need to have another man push his cock into Rusty's ass. Even though being gay wasn't necessarily accepted on the bull riding circuit, it wasn't really ostracized either. Well, maybe a little. Certain guys you avoided, but what you did in your hotel room was your own business, just don't flaunt it, and don't come onto your fellow riders.

Thus his dilemma. He couldn't come out to his family, and he couldn't approach the guy he wanted.

Lucas Jacks.

Even the guy's name sent shivers down Rusty's back. The man was six foot of pure muscle, big blue eyes, and blond hair. He could fill out a pair of Wranglers like nobody's business and make it look easy. When he rode, every muscle is his body flexed with fluid motion like ripples on a pond. Rusty loved to watch Lucas ride, but what he wanted more was to have Lucas ride him.

Rusty blew out a breath as his guy's name hit the screen. He was the last to ride in this final round for the win in Oklahoma City. Rusty watched as Lucas eased himself down on the back of the bull. The bull jumped. Rusty held his breath as the spotter pulled Lucas up by his vest. The bull finally settled down inside the chute and Lucas could get his wrap in place.

The moment Lucas gave the nod, Rusty's stomach knotted. Bull riding was a dangerous sport no matter how you looked at it. Being on the back of something that didn't want you there was suicide in most people's eyes, but they loved it. Being a bull rider was a constant adrenaline high from the time you psyched yourself up for the ride, until the moment you released your hand after your eight seconds, and for some time after that. People called them adrenaline junkies, and they probably were. Nothing could compare to that high, at least nothing he'd found yet.

The buzzer sounded. Lucas made eight seconds. Rusty rubbed his stomach to ease the tenseness as he watched Lucas run for the fence with the bull hot on his heels. The railing made a loud *clang* as the bull hit his head against it right between Lucas's spread legs.

The bull fighters got the animal's attention, leading him away from Lucas and into the exit chute. Lucas climbed down before looking up at where Rusty knew the score board flashed his numbers. The announcer called out the results as they flashed on the screen. "What the hell? He was robbed! That was at least an eighty-nine point ride! Eight-six is crazy."

The door to his room banged against the wall as his brothers Thomas and William, or Junior as they called him, came barreling into the room. Both boys skidded to a halt at the edge of the bed, there boots sliding on the hardwood. "You're home!"

"Yeah."

"We saw your ride even though Mom and Dad don't like us watching. The bull stepped right on you."

"Yes he did."

"Does your leg hurt?" William asked, eyeing the cast.

"Yep."

"Wow. How long are you going to be off the circuit?" Thomas moved closer, holding out his hand to touch the cast. "Can I sign it?"

"I'm done for the season and yes, you can sign it in a couple of days. It's still a bit soft since they just put it on yesterday."

"Out for the season, that sucks." William stood at the side of the bed, his eyes wide with wonder. "Who won today?"

"Levi did."

"Awesome! I like him. I'd sure like to meet him one day."

"I'll see what I can arrange."

"Really? That would be so cool! He's a great rider."

"Yes he is and he's a friend."

Thomas picked at the lint ball on the bed, his eyes focused on the television screen as they awarded the buckle to Levi. "You have a lot of cool friends."

"Boys, lunch is ready!"

"Can we eat with Rusty?"

"No, you eat at the table. Your brother isn't going anywhere. You can talk to him after you eat. Come on, now."

William turned and headed for the door, leaving Thomas behind for a moment. "I'm glad you're home even if it's only for a little while."

"I'll be here at least eight weeks, Thomas. That's two months."

Thomas scuffed his boot against the floor. "I miss you when you're gone."

"I miss you guys too."

"Thomas!"

"Comin', Ma." Thomas turned and headed for the door before glancing back over his shoulder. "Can we maybe play cards or somethin' later?"

"Sure, buddy."

Thomas grinned before he walked out the door to get lunch in the kitchen. Rusty really did love his family, all of them, but Thomas had a special place in his heart as the youngest. Thomas had been born premature at only one pound, eight ounces. They didn't think he would survive when he'd first been born because of heart problems, breathing problems, and he wouldn't eat very well, but his little brother proved them all wrong. Even though he wasn't the biggest kid in his class, he was by far the smartest of all of them, getting straight As in school. His kid brother wanted to fly planes for a living and even go into space. If anyone could do it, it was Thomas.

Several minutes later, his mother came in carrying a tray loaded down with spaghetti, meatballs, a huge glass of milk, and several slices of bread.

"Wow. I'm going to have to diet while I'm here. You'll have me weighing three hundred pounds with all this food."

"You eat what you want, Rusty. You are by far too thin anyway."

"I need to watch my weight, Ma. They don't have heavy bull riders. Most of us are small, thin, and wiry." He put the tray across his lap and dug in. Nothing like his mother's spaghetti. It was one of his favorite meals and he would probably eat every last bit of the food on his plate. He hadn't realized how hungry he was until he smelled it. "I love your food."

She brushed a kiss on the top of his head. "I know you do. Eat up." She stepped away from the side of the bed. "I'll be back to get your plate in a bit."

"Go eat. You need your strength to keep up with all of us."

"True." She turned to head out into the hall, but stopped to glance at the television screen. "Who won this week?"

"Levi."

"Good. He seems like a nice man."

Rusty frowned. "I didn't know you watched, Ma."

"I watch every week, Rusty. My boy is on there. I may not understand it all, but I watch." She smiled, giving him a sly wink. "Besides, it pisses your dad off because I let Thomas and William see the show with me."

Rusty laughed. It was the first real laugh he'd had in several days, and it felt good. Maybe coming home for a short time wasn't such a bad idea.

"Rusty!" He woke from his nap with a start at the yelling coming from his doorway.

"What?" he shouted back as he propped himself back up against the headboard with his hands.

"You're sleeping like an old woman?" Russell snickered from his place next to the end of the bed.

Darkness had fallen sometime while he slept. His room was pitch-black except for the small light on the nightstand next to his bed. His stomach rumbled. He'd slept several hours from the pain pill he'd taken earlier. *Great. I'll be up all night now probably.* "What the hell do you want, Russell?"

"I stopped to see how you are since chores are done for the day."

"I'm fine."

"You look busted up."

"I am. The bull fractured my femur. I'll be in this cast for several weeks."

"Figures. Getting out of work…again."

"Yeah, blow it out your ass, Russell. I work when I'm home."

Russell glanced down at the cast on Rusty's leg. "How long are you going to be here?"

"Eight weeks or more. It depends on how it's healing."

"So you're out for the rest of the season?"

"Yep, so you'll have me here until we start up again in January."

"Well, la-te-da."

"What's your problem?"

"You. Don't think you can come back here and take over stuff because you're the eldest. I run this show now, me and Dad. You are just another hand around here when you work."

"Dad gave you the foreman job?"

"Yeah. Why wouldn't he? You don't care about this place, unlike me. This is my life's blood, my future."

"You can have it, Russell. I don't want it. I'll ride until I can't ride anymore, then I'll put more stock on my place, get it running better before I see about raising a family."

"Where do you plan to raise this family, Rusty? Here in Albuquerque?"

"Of course. I have my own ranch to do it on, besides, what difference does it make? I'll live my life how I want to."

He moved his hand, waving it back and forth between them. "Just so we're clear."

"No worries, brother. I'm out of commission for several weeks. I won't be bossing anyone around since I probably won't be out of this bed for a day or two without crutches."

"See that you don't."

"Don't think you're calling the shots with me, Russell. I don't take orders from you even if you are the foreman now."

"You'll do what I say if you're on the back of a horse after that cast comes off."

"No, I'll do what Dad says and remember, I'm still the eldest."

"Not by much."

"Enough."

"What like fifteen minutes?"

"Fifteen minutes is fifteen minutes."

"You left us to follow your dream of riding bulls, Rusty. I stayed to run the ranch. It will be mine when all is said and done."

"You go on thinking whatever you want to think. Dad and Mom will decide who gets the home place, not you."

"Dad resents you leaving."

"I know he does, but it's my life."

"Then you live your life how you want. Leave the ranching to me." Russell spun on his heels and disappeared through the door.

Rusty hated fighting with his twin, but it was what it was. They'd always fought, even from the time they were little. Russell hated the fact that Rusty was the eldest and always seemed to find favor with his parents no matter what the situation. No, they weren't identical. In fact, their personalities were totally different. Rusty was quiet and unobtrusive where Russell was in your face, constantly fighting for more, and being a jerk most of the time. Rusty wished his brother would calm down and quit being so competitive over the home place. As it stood, even if his parents gave him the ranch when they passed on, he'd give it to his brother. He had his own plans.

His mother stopped in the doorway on her way down the hall from the laundry room. "Do you have clothes to wash, Rusty?"

"Yes, in my gear bag. Most everything I own is dirty. I hadn't had a chance to wash before I came home."

"It's fine, honey. I know how it goes." She set the basket in her arms on the floor near his bag and rustled through the duffle, leaving a small cloud of dirt and the smell of bulls in the air. "Wow. What a stench."

"Sorry."

"It's fine. Nothing different that your brothers when they come in from branding."

"Cattle or bulls, they both smell similar."

She laughed. "Yes, yes they do."

After she had his dirty clothes in the basket, she walked to the doorway and turned around. "Supper will be ready in about an hour. Did you sleep well?"

"Yeah, but now I'll be up all night probably. Those pain pills make me sleepy, but now I'm wide awake."

"Can you make it to the dining room for supper?"

"Yeah. I need to get up and move a bit before I go stir crazy in this room."

"I can imagine."

"I'll work my way in there in a little bit. I need to use the restroom."

"You know where it is and no worries. You don't have to share it with anyone."

"Thanks, Mom."

"You're welcome. See you at dinner."

He eyed the crutches propped at the end of his bed. He could do this. He moved his leg so it dangled off the side of the bed, inhaling sharply when it began to throb relentlessly. Pain pills were a must, but he hated taking them so often since they just made him sleep a lot. Life would go on while he slept and it probably would help him heal. He would regret missing anything that happened over the next few months though.

With the crutches beneath his arms, he tried rocking to get himself to his feet. It didn't work. He'd have to call for help. "Thomas?"

A minute later, Thomas came skidding to a halt in the doorway. His brother loved to do that Risky Business slide. "What's up?"

"Can you help me to my feet? I'm headed into the dining room for supper."

"Ma said it wouldn't be ready for an hour."

"That's okay. It'll probably take me that long to hobble in there, but I can't get my ass off the bed."

"What do you want me to do?"

"Get under my arm and hoist me to my feet."

"Are you sure I can carry you?"

"I just need your shoulders to help me. Bend at the knees and push. I should be able to get up."

"Okay."

After a couple of tries, he managed to climb up and balance on his one foot while the toes of his casted leg barely touched the floor. They'd said no weight bearing until he went in two weeks from now to see how the leg was healing.

"Good?"

"Yeah, but walk behind me so in case I fall, I can land on you."

"Ha, ha. Very funny."

"Just walk behind me. You can steady me if I get wobbly."

"All right, but no falling on me. You'll break me in half."

"You're a good sized kid for sixteen. You'll be fine."

"Thanks a lot."

As he made his way out into the hall, he slowly worked his good leg with the crutches under his arms, until he made it to the opening of the dining room. He was out of breath and pouring sweat. "Damn, this is killing me."

"You're out of shape, Rusty." Thomas laughed.

"I can hang on for eight seconds on the back of a raging bull, but walking on crutches five hundred feet is wearing my ass out."

"Rusty, I've told you about the language."

"Sorry, Ma."

"Take a seat where you normally sit. I'll get you a glass of sweet tea to tide you over until dinner."

"I need something. My mouth feels like I've been chewing on cotton balls for the last several hours."

"It's all the snoring you were doing," Thomas said.

"I don't snore."

"You apparently do. It sounded like a sleeping bear in there."

Rusty punched Thomas in the arm. "Don't you have work to do?"

"Nope." Thomas slid into the chair to Rusty's right. "I'm done for the day."

"I'm sure something needs to be fed, stalls need to be cleaned, or something. Right, Mom?"

She shook her head as she peeled potatoes at the sink. "He's done. You're stuck with him until he has to go to bed and being Saturday, he doesn't have to be in there until later than normal."

"Well crap."

Thomas laughed as he set up a game of dominoes on the table. "We can play a few games while supper is cooking."

"I'll beat the pants off you."

"No you won't."

"Game on, brother, game on."

He would have weeks of healing to do before he could even contemplate getting back on a bull, but his target would be making it to finals. He wanted to see who came out on top this year.

Chapter Two

Lucas Jacks watched from the side lines as Levi Bond took home the buckle, the million bucks, and the World Championship title. *It should have been Rusty's.* He felt bad. Rusty should have been the one out there. Life wasn't fair and Rusty had been given his share of shit lately.

He glanced to his right where several of his fellow bull riders lined the fence for the awards ceremony. Rusty had flown in for the last several rides of the finals, his leg freshly healed from the break of several weeks ago. He still favored the limb a little and Lucas worried he wouldn't be back when the circuit resumed in January. Lucas couldn't imagine the circuit without Rusty on it and to have him go out like that would kill the moral of the group. No one wanted to go out with a permanent injury.

Rusty rubbed his leg before taking the seat behind him. Lucas frowned. He could tell his friend was in pain and it bothered him. Who was he kidding, he was into Rusty Arnold, big time, although he sure didn't know which way Rusty swung.

It really didn't matter. Rusty was out of his league.

"What's up, Lucas?" A leggy, long haired blonde leaned over the railing right above him.

She looked familiar to him, but he couldn't quite place her. "Nothing much. What's up with you?"

"Nothing. Would you like to hang out with me after the ceremony? I'm headed to the bar here in the hotel."

"Uh, sure, I guess."

She laughed, smacking him in the shoulder. "You don't remember me, do you?"

"Sorry, but no."

"Pamela. Pamela Reardon. Butch's sister?"

"Oh. Yeah, sure. You aren't hanging out with Butch?"

"No. He's busy scoping things out for himself. He doesn't want his little sister hanging out with him, I'm sure." She smoothed her hand over his shoulder and down his bicep. "I'll even let you buy me a drink."

"Are you old enough to drink?"

She smacked his arm. "I'm legal in more ways than one, honey."

"Well then. I just might buy you one after all." He watched Rusty struggle to his feet without bending too much. He wanted to help him, but he figured it wouldn't be well received. "I need to grab my stuff from the back. Meet me at the bar, and I'll buy you a beer, for Butch's sake."

Her nose crinkled up as she frowned. "Okay."

Lucas went through the dirt arena to the locker rooms in the back, grabbed his gear bag and went back through the long walkway to the seats. He really wanted to check on Rusty, but he figured the other man had already left. He was shocked to find him still sitting back in the seat where he'd been before.

He tipped his hat back on his head and said, "Hey, Rusty."

Rusty's head spun toward him. "Oh, hey, Lucas. What's up?"

"You okay?"

"Yeah, just resting the leg before I make my way to the bar to celebrate with you guys. You did well, my friend."

"Not well enough. Levi took home the buckle."

"I know, but you placed in a good spot."

"Money is money, I guess." He slid into the seat next to Rusty. "I'm sorry you got bumped out by the break. How is your leg?"

"Still hurts some. I'll be back next year though."

"You should have won this year. You were riding at the top of your game. Having to go out like that must have sucked."

"Yeah, but it's not a career ending injury."

"Good thing. I would hate to see you out permanently."

"Thanks."

"I heard breaks like yours take surgery. Did you have to do that?"

"Yeah, about two weeks after the break, they had to surgically fix it with a plate even though the break was pretty clean and straight."

"You really think you'll be back in January?"

"That's my plan, but we'll see. Doctor's don't seem to think so. They say four to six months to heal properly. You know bull riders though, we are suckers for punishment."

"I know what you mean, but you should let it heal completely before trying to come back, Rusty, otherwise you could do some real damage."

"I know. I'm playing it by ear. I have doctor appointments set up for every month. I won't come back before the doctor says it's healed. I won't be able to dismount with it the way it is right now."

"Well, since we don't restart until January, that'll be about four months."

"I know."

Lucas took the chair two seats down. "How are things at the home place?"

"Good. My brothers are handling things on my parent's ranch and my foreman is holding down mine. Russell is being a pain in the ass since Dad made him foreman on their place."

"He did?"

"Yep, when Jack retired about six months ago."

Lucas remembered growing up in the same town as Rusty's family. They had been friends for several years now after they'd both starting mutton busting on the local rodeo circuit, and then graduating to bulls when they got to their high school years. Lucas always knew he was gay, but he and Rusty never discussed those things. They were friends, yes, but not close enough to talk about sexual preferences. They'd both had girlfriends in high school. His was mostly to cover up his attraction to guys, Rusty, he wasn't so sure about. Days turned into years and his attraction to his friend never wavered, although he was sure Rusty didn't return the fascination.

"I'm glad Levi won. He deserved it," Rusty said, running his hand down his thigh.

"No, you deserved it, but if anyone should take it away from you, I'm glad it was Levi."

"I appreciate it." Rusty sat forward, grasped the bar to the railing and hauled himself to his feet. "I'm ready for that beer."

"Me too."

As they started slowly climbing the steps to exit the arena, Rusty said, "I saw you talking to Butch's sister, Pamela. You hooking up for the night?"

"Nope."

"Why not? She's kind of cute."

"And a fellow rider's sister. There is an unwritten rule, remember? We don't fuck family members."

"True, but she wants you, man."

"I know. I told her I'd buy her a beer, but that's as far as it goes." Lucas watched as his friend made his way up the stairs. He'd make sure nothing happened to Rusty. "What about you? You hooking up with someone?"

"Nah. This bum legs makes it damned hard to fuck anyone at the moment."

"I bet."

They made it to the top of the seats and worked their way down the hall out into the main area of the arena.

"Where are you parked?"

"With the rider's vehicles. Even though I wasn't participating, I convinced them to let me park there."

"They should. You should have been down behind the chutes, man."

"I went down there for a little bit, but with it being so packed and everything it was bothering my leg, so I went back to my seat. Hell, I was lucky enough to get the one I bought even if I did have to buy it from a scalper."

"The hell you say! I would have given you my family ticket. None of mine even came."

"I hadn't thought of it." Rusty shrugged. "No problem. I had an awesome seat. The family seats aren't usually the best."

"I bet you paid one hell of a price for that ticket."

He nodded. "You can say that again, but it was worth it for the view. I could even smell the sweat on the guys as they rode."

Their conversation lagged as they walked out the back door to the rear parking area. Only their two vehicles remained besides the huge trailers loading the bulls and the big semi's loading the equipment. World Finals was over. The season was done until January now, giving Rusty time to heal before it started all over in New York City.

The bar over at the hotel is where everyone would hang out, get drunk, pick up women, and cause general mayhem. It sounded good to Lucas. "I'll meet you at the bar?"

"Sounds good."

Lucas watched Rusty get into his truck gingerly, start the vehicle and then pull out before he cranked over the engine on his own.

When he pulled into the bar parking lot a few minutes later, he was shocked to see so many people. Women and men both, hung around outside on the patio where they smoked and drank. He could imagine the crowd inside. If people wanted to rub elbows with the bull riders, this was the place to do it.

Rusty had pulled in a few spots down with his rental vehicle.

Lucas locked his door after he got out, slamming it shut as a couple of people waved from the patio.

"Hey Lucas! Grab a beer and joins us."

"Thanks."

He met Rusty at the door as they made their way inside. The place was packed. Your typical honky-tonk sported a long bar with hundreds of types of liquor. They had beer on tap, beer in the bottle, and every kind of alcohol you could imagine in rows and rows of bottles behind the bar.

Hundreds of cowboy hats lined every inch of the place. Everything from straw hats to fancy Stetsons graced every head. Rhinestones twinkled in the flashing lights from the dance floor. Music blared from the speakers. If he guessed right, the DJ was playing top forty hits. A Jason Aldean song rattled them with the heavy base. Peanut shells crunched under boots as people walked around. All in all, it was a hell of a set up. This place bled country.

They found an empty spot at the bar and signaled for the bartender.

"What'll ya have?"

"Beer...Rusty?"

"Sure."

"Two MGD in the bottle, please."

"Comin' right up."

As soon as their beers appeared, Lucas swung around, brought the bottle to his lips, and took a long draw. The malty liquid eased down his throat in a cold slide straight to his stomach. "Ah. That's good."

"Yep."

He made small talk with Rusty as best he could with the music so loud. Pamela came in, nodded, and then made her way to the other end of the bar. *Weird.* He turned to watch where she went, noticing Butch standing not two cowboy hats down from him. No wonder she made a beeline for the other end of the bar. She probably wanted to hook up with someone, had her sights set on him, but when she noticed Butch right there, she decided to find other prey. Fine with him. She wasn't his type anyway.

They stayed for several hours, mostly people watching. Some guys left with buckle bunnies, some left together, and some left alone. He often wondered how many on the circuit really were gay and kept it hidden from everyone. He knew of a few.

He didn't see Levi hanging out at the bar, but then again, he hadn't expected to. He'd heard his traveling partner, Curt Walsh, had taken a blow to the head in a bar fight a couple of days ago, and now lay in the hospital. He hoped everything turned out okay with Curt.

Tomorrow they would be back on the road for home. He should ask Rusty if he wanted to ride home with him although he probably would do better flying. He could stretch his leg out a bit on the plane rather than be cramped up in the cab of his truck. He'd ask anyway. He leaned in to get close to Rusty's ear. The cologne Rusty wore tore at his senses in the most delicious way, and he found himself breathing deeply, inhaling the scent so it wrapped around his head.

"Are you sniffing me?"

"Sorry. I like the scent you're wearing. What is it?"

When Rusty told him, he made a mental note to buy some just so he could smell it and think of Rusty. How sick was that? "I wanted to ask you if you'd rather ride home with me or take your plane ride."

"I'd better fly. I'm in first class so I can stretch out my leg."

"No problem. Just thought I'd ask."

"Is there anyone else going our way?"

"Not that doesn't have their vehicle here too." He shrugged. "It's fine. I'll put on some music, kick back with the cruise control, and jam out all the way home."

"Are you sure you don't want to hook up with some girl? I don't want to hold you back by making you stand here and talk to me."

"I'd rather talk to you."

Rusty did a double take as he brought his beer to his lips, draining the remainder in a few gulps.

Did that come off as a come on?

"Listen, Lucas. Maybe we should talk. Let's go someplace quiet."

Lucas's heart dropped to his stomach. Was this really happening? Were they going to talk like he thought they were going to talk? How would he broach the subject? Could he come right out and say, 'Hey, Rusty, I think you're hot, and I want to fuck you right into tomorrow morning?' He wasn't sure he could, but it seemed they were going to get some things out in the open tonight. The thought scared the hell out of him.

They put their bottles down on the bar and paid their tab before he followed Rusty's slow gait outside.

"Are you staying at the hotel by the arena?" Rusty asked.

"Yeah."

"Me too. Let's talk in my room."

"Are you sure you want to do that?"

"Yes. I think we need some privacy, don't you?"

"Uh, yeah, I guess so." He removed his hat before he shoved his hand through his hair. "How about I stop at the corner market and get a half rack? I think I'm going to need a drink."

"Sounds good. I'm in four-twenty-eight on the fourth floor. Meet me there."

"Okay."

Lucas headed for his truck. Luckily, they'd only drank a couple of beers while they were at the bar, so he and Rusty were both okay to drive back to the hotel, but even if he'd had more, the thought of having this conversation would have sobered him right up. He pulled up to the twenty-four hour quickie mart, ran inside, and bought some beer. He almost wished he would have bought something stronger, but yeah, beer would have to do.

He had a feeling this would be one strange night.

* * * *

Rusty sat in the chair near the window in his room as he waited for Lucas to knock on the door. Sweat coated his palms. His heart thumped loudly and rapidly in his chest. He felt dizzy with anticipation. This was it. He was ready to tell Lucas about his attraction to him and see what happened? Yeah, he really was. He'd planned this talk over in his head so many times, he knew the lines by heart.

They'd grown up together, which was the weird part, but they'd never really talked about guy things like guys do. Women and sex never came up in their conversations as teenagers. Not that they were particularly close, but Lucas had spent time at Rusty's parents place and vice versa. They'd slept in the same room together several times, talking about bull riding, rodeo, horses, and ranching, but never about women. He wondered why it never came up.

His attraction for Lucas had been there for a long time, even way back in high school, but you didn't admit to being gay back then. Hell no. If you did, you would have been ostracized, beaten up, laughed at, and called every kind of name from faggot to queer.

A soft knock sounded on the door. Rusty wiped his palms on the thighs of his jeans, struggled to his feet, and moved toward the door. He blew out a nervous breath. This was it. Their talk might change everything between them or nothing at all.

He opened the door. The man of his wet dreams stood in front of him still dressed in his cowboy finery, from his button-down shirt, to his Wrangler jeans, dusty cowboy boots, and black Stetson.

"Can I come in? I brought beer." Lucas held up the twelve pack of Budweiser he bought.

"Uh, sorry. Come on in." Rusty stepped back to allow him to enter, and when Lucas walked past, Rusty realized the scent he wore was something he'd come to realize was uniquely Lucas, a dark, musky smell he would forever associate with the man he wanted to fuck with everything inside him. "You can put that on the table by the window if you want. Is it cold?"

"Yeah. I grabbed it out of the refrigerator section."

"Good. There's a fridge down below there to keep them in."

"Great thinking."

Rusty shrugged. "It was already here."

He took a seat on the bed as Lucas put a couple of beers in the refrigerator. His jeans pulled tight across his ass, making Rusty's mouth water. *Good grief, I'm going to die here.* He swallowed hard, almost choking on the saliva pooling in his mouth. *It's really warm in here.* "You can sit in the chair over there if you want to."

"Sounds good."

Silence enveloped them as the air thickened with tension. Rusty struggled to figure out what to say to Lucas to make him understand the attraction he'd harbored for his friend for so long, he couldn't remember when it started exactly.

Lucas took a long draw on his beer as Rusty did the same, his foot nervously tapping out an imaginary rhythm on the carpeted floor.

"I'm gay," they both blurted out at the same time.

Lucas's eyes widened. "You are?"

"Yeah. I have been for a long time. I didn't realize you were."

"Yep, since I figured out there was a difference between boys and girls."

"What about Stephanie in high school?"

"That was to cover up the fact I wanted to be with a guy." Lucas sipped his beer for a couple minutes before he said, "What about you? You went out with Andrea for a couple of years."

"I was trying to figure out what I wanted. Would you believe I never slept with her? We did some heavy petting, but never got down to anything hardcore like actual penetration and I found it almost impossible to get a hard on with her. I had to imagine I was with someone else to even get off when she gave me a blow job."

"Wow." The reverent whisper sent chills down Rusty's spine.

"So how many guys have you been with?" Lucas asked, his fingers now dangling between his parted knees.

Rusty shrugged. He didn't think it was that important, but he answered the question anyway. "Several. I usually try to get my rocks off on the road with guys who aren't fellow riders. They are kind of weirded out by gay guys being in the same locker room they are. What about you?"

"I usually wait until I get home."

Rusty's heart hammered in his chest. He had to ask the burning question on his tongue or he'd never know. "Are you in a steady relationship?"

"Nope." Lucas raised his head to meet Rusty's stare across the small expanse of the room. "Although, I did think I was in love with someone once, but he didn't want anything serious." Lucas took another sip of his beer. "You?"

Rusty's stomach knotted. Did he admit he'd been in a relationship in the past that had turned sour after the other man cheated on him with a mutual friend? "No. Not currently."

"But you have been in the past?"

"Yeah. It didn't end well."

"I'm sorry. That must have sucked."

"It did. We were together for what I would consider a long time. Two years."

"Were you riding then?"

"No, it was before I started bull riding professionally."

"Did it happen in our hometown?"

"Yes. Albuquerque isn't that small so it's fairly easy to hide a gay relationship."

Lucas shrugged. "True. I can usually find someone to fuck when I'm home. I haven't tried to be out about my gay status though."

"I'm not open about mine either."

"Do your parents know?"

"Hell no. Neither do my brothers." Rusty drained the rest of his beer before pulling his legs under him the best he could to get to his feet for another one out of the box. Lucas leaned forward, handing him another. "What about your parents?"

"My sister knows, but no, my parents and brother don't know. They wouldn't understand at all. They would totally disown me."

Rusty popped the top on the beer can, sending a small spurt of beer onto the carpet. "Yeah, mine would too. My dad is already preaching about me quitting the circuit, coming home, and running the ranch. Russell is all over me because my dad made him foreman. He thinks his shit don't stink now. I heard it every day while I was recuperating. It sucked."

"I can imagine. How are the younger boys doing? They idolize you, you know."

The malty liquid slid down his throat in a wash of goodness as he tipped the can to his lips. "Yeah. They hung around a lot while I was laid up wanting stories of the road, rides, crashes, and gossip."

"They are good kids. How old are they now?"

"Thomas is fifteen and Junior is sixteen."

"They are growing so fast."

"Yeah, it was kind of weird that Mom had two more kids after me and Russell were already half grown, but to each his own, I guess."

"We never know about parents anymore." Lucas laughed before finishing off his can. "My sister is getting married soon."

"Is she? I didn't realize she was seeing anyone seriously."

"Yeah. She's known him quite a long time. They've been dating for about a year. The wedding is next summer."

"Cool."

They sat in silence for a few minutes while Lucas studied Rusty's face. Rusty didn't know what to make of the look until Lucas blurted out, "Wanna fuck?"

Chapter Three

Lucas smiled as Rusty choked on his beer, shock written across his face. He kind of liked shocking his friend, but he'd like to fuck him more, right between the ass cheeks or have him suck him off. That would be good too. *I'm getting horny just thinking about it. That's something that hasn't happened in a bit. Too many of my hookups lately have been boring. I don't think Rusty will be boring at all.*

"What did you say?" Rusty put his beer on the floor.

His hands appeared to be shaking with excitement or at least Lucas hoped it was excitement.

"I asked if you want to fuck. I've been attracted to you for a long time, but since I didn't know you were gay, I didn't want to push the envelope. Now that I'm aware of your sexual preferences, I want to bury my cock deep in your ass." He shrugged. "So, do you wanna fuck?"

"Wow." Rusty wiped his hands on the thighs of his jeans. "Yeah, I want to fuck you. I mean, I have for a long time—since high school."

"We really should have talked before now."

"Yeah, but now is good." Rusty climbed to his feet, his leg looking like it was stiff and difficult to maneuver.

"You sure this is going to work with your leg? You look uncomfortable." Lucas stood, his concern for his friend taking precedence over his hard on.

"I'll be fine." Rusty began unbuttoning his shirt, slipping the material over his shoulders a moment later.

Lucas liked to look. He had a little bit of a voyeur tendency, so watching Rusty strip was turning him on more than he could even fathom. Rusty had a firm chest with a bit of dark chest hair sprinkled across his pecs. His abs were firm and ripped from riding bulls. When he toed off his boots, and then stripped off his jeans, Lucas almost groaned out loud. His thighs and calves were rock solid from gripping the side of the bull as he rode.

Lucas couldn't wait to feel those thighs wrapped around his waist as he buried himself deep. His cock ached with need, leaking a bit of pre-cum out the end. His balls hurt too, from the desire to bury himself so deep in Rusty's ass, they would both be walking a little gingerly in the morning.

"Aren't you going to take your clothes off?"

"I like watching you."

Rusty stood in front of him naked as the day he was born, his cock hard, long, and proud standing straight up. Lucas's mouth watered to taste as he watched a bit of pre-cum glisten on the tip of Rusty's cock.

"You look like you want to eat me alive."

"I do. I want to take your entire length in my mouth."

Rusty sucked in a ragged breath. "Do it. I would love to feel your sexy mouth around my cock."

Lucas dropped to his knees on the floor in front of Rusty, palming his balls in a firm grip, one meant to bring the other man pleasure with a little pain.

When he sucked just the head of Rusty's cock between his lips, Rusty sighed. "Holy hell."

Rusty buried his fingers in Lucas's hair, pulling his head closer. Lucas tipped his head back a little, opening his jaw so he could take Rusty's length. The scent surrounding his senses, made him harder than he ever thought possible. Musk, sex, and male arousal penetrated his nose. Good God, he loved that smell.

Lucas bobbed his head, sucking, licking, doing the best job at giving head he'd ever managed. He wanted Rusty to enjoy this first time so there would be lots more in the coming weeks. The thought of having Rusty as a steady fuck buddy had Lucas envisioning all the things they could try. He sure hoped Rusty was adventurous in the bedroom because thoughts of tying him up, fucking his mouth, burying himself in Rusty's ass, and fucking him against the wall made Lucas hurt from the desire racing through him. He never thought in a million years he and Rusty would be doing this, but he was going to take advantage of it for however long it lasted.

Rusty groaned as Lucas continued to suck. He wanted Rusty to come in his mouth. He wanted to taste the essence of his friend on his tongue.

When Rusty let out a low pitched, lusty growl and shot cum down Lucas's throat, he swallowed every bit of the milky liquid on his tongue like a dying man.

Rusty collapsed back on the bed, effectively pulling his softening cock from Lucas's mouth. "That was fantastic."

"I'm glad you enjoyed yourself." Lucas quickly removed his own clothing, stripping down to bare skin in about six seconds flat. He wanted this, wanted it badly.

Lucas looked down as he palmed his own aching cock. The head was purple, glistening, and looked painful. It wasn't...much, but he wanted to push it deep inside Rusty more than anything. "Do you have lube?"

"Yeah, in my gear bag next to the rosin."

Lucas walked to the dresser, found Rusty's gear bag next to it and rummaged through it until he located the tube of lubrication they would need. No dry slides tonight. He wanted all the pleasure with no pain for their first time. Dry sliding just hurt all the way around, no matter which end you were on. "How do you want to do this? Your comfort is paramount here with your leg."

Rusty lifted his head from the supine position he'd taken on the bed. "How about over the side? I can roll on my stomach with my legs dangling off the end of the bed. That way I don't have to put pressure on my leg."

"Sounds good. Roll over and spread those ass cheeks, I'm coming in for the ride." Lucas grabbed a condom out of his pants pocket, rolled it down his cock, and prepared himself for the ride of his life.

Rusty rolled over, slid down so his hips sat on the edge of the bed, his legs dangling off the side, and his ass in the air. The sight made Lucas sigh with pleasure.

He slicked up his cock with the lube from Rusty's bag before sending a dollop down between Rusty's ass cheeks. With two fingers, he worked the lube into his friend's tissues, spreading it around his hole and into the sensitive area just inside. When everything seemed slick and pliable, he positioned the head of his cock at the puckered hole and slowly pushed inside. Rusty sighed, relaxing all his muscles, allowing Lucas to fully penetrate his ass.

The sensation was incredible.

Rusty's ass fit him like a glove, a soft, warm, tight glove.

"Oh God." Rusty sighed. "That's fabulous. So fucking fantastic, I can hardly hold still. Move, now, please."

Lucas began the slow glide of his cock in and out of Rusty's ass. He shivered as he felt his cock burn from need so strong, he thought he might die right there.

His fingers dug into Rusty's hips as he shoved himself balls deep. The grip of Rusty's anal channel drove his desire higher. His balls drew up, waiting for him to allow them to explode. He continued to shove his cock deeper and deeper until he felt the hair on his groin brush the back of Rusty's ass. Being as deep as he could go, Lucas felt goose bumps raise the hair on his arms as he lost control over his own desire and came hard enough to see stars. "Fuck!"

"Oh yeah. That's it."

Lucas pumped a few more times, milking his orgasm for all it was worth before his legs gave out and he collapsed on the bed beside Rusty. "Holy hell."

"You can say that again."

Sweat dripped from his temple, sliding down until he wiped it away with a weak hand. "Sweet baby Jesus."

Rusty rolled onto his side and propped his head up with his hand. Lucas turned his head to look into his friend's eyes. He liked what he saw. Contentment battled for lust in Rusty's gaze.

"I hope you enjoyed that as much as I did."

"Hell yeah."

"Good. We can do it again then."

"You bet."

Rusty reached over and grasped Lucas's soft cock in his hand. "Next time, I want your ass."

"Sure. I'd like that."

"I'm glad you said so because I've been dreaming about it for a long time." Rusty sat up, grabbed his pants from the floor, and started to slip them gingerly over his feet. "Right now. I want some food. There is a little restaurant that looked like an all-night diner, next door. How about we get something to eat and then come back here for more sex?"

"Sounds like a plan to me."

Lucas got to his feet and quickly dressed watching Rusty for signs he was too rough with his friend.

Rusty moved slowly, but didn't seem worse for wear from their sexual escapades, so Lucas let the feeling of protectiveness slide off his shoulders. He couldn't worry. He didn't have the right, really, but they were friends even if that friendship had turned to lovers for the time being.

"Are you headed home tomorrow?" Rusty asked as they made their way down the hall of the hotel a few minutes later.

"Yeah. With finals over, I need to get home and get some work done."

"Didn't you get a degree in something before you started riding bulls?"

"Yep. I actually teach at the high school during my off time. History was my major in college."

"Wow. A history teacher."

"Part-time or substitute is what I do when I can. Usually on our downtime, which isn't much these days with all the invitationals and stuff going on."

Rusty pulled open the door to the diner a few minutes later, a small bell banging against the glass announcing their arrival. "I know what you mean."

They found a booth to their right in the corner. Lucas liked to be able to watch the door. It appeared a few of their rider buddies had found this place too as they passed several guys in a couple of booths. After a few hellos and chin tips from their fellow riders, he and Rusty slid into the booth on opposite sides facing each other.

The waitress came over and took their drink order as they looked over the menu. Not terribly hungry, Lucas decided on a piece of pie with ice cream and a cup of coffee. He had no idea what Rusty might want or how hungry he was. He let his glance take in his friend turned lover. Rusty had dark hair that he wore kind of long as it brushed his collar, green eyes with eyelashes long enough to make a woman jealous, a wide chest with muscles on muscles, big hands, a trim abdomen, nice cock, long legs, and some awesome riding abilities.

Rusty had made riding bulls look easy even when they were in high school. It was no wonder he'd been on top of the circuit before his accident. Unfortunately, that kind of thing happened a lot. Riders rode many times with broken bones, dislocated shoulders, broken ribs, concussions, and even worse injuries. It was part of who they were, adrenaline junkies.

Lucas looked over Rusty's shoulder to take in their fellow riders at the other tables. He recognized several of them, Jefferson Thompson, Butch Reardon, J.M. Moneymaker, Carl Whistler, Robert Johns, C.B. Parker, and Stewart Collins. The best of the best graced this little diner with their presence tonight, probably hoping no one would recognize them so they didn't have to play the crowd. It was something they had to deal with, but sometimes they just wanted to be normal folks.

"What?" Rusty looked over his shoulder.

"Nothing. Just noticing who was sitting at the other tables."

"I should have said hi to them. I haven't seen most of them in the couple of months since my accident."

"Why don't you go over there for a minute? I can order whatever you want."

Rusty slid out of the booth, gingerly getting to his feet. "Okay. Order me a cheeseburger, some fries, and a Coke." He tipped his hat before taking the several steps to the other guys' table.

Lucas could hear their conversation clearly, but he still turned so he could see the group.

"How're you feeling, Rusty?" Carl asked.

"Good. A little stiff with the leg."

"You gonna be back in January?" Butch sipped his drink, giving Rusty a nod.

"That's the plan."

"You should have taken the championship. Levi didn't deserve it," Jefferson snapped, making Lucas frown. Jefferson obviously didn't like Levi very well for some reason.

"Levi rode hella good for the last several months. He did deserve the championship, Jefferson. You're bitter because you didn't do very well."

Lucas smiled, listening to Rusty stand up for Levi.

"Didn't you hear?"

"Hear what?"

"He's fuckin' Curt Walsh."

"So. What's your point, Jefferson? Jealous?"

"Hell yeah, I'm jealous. Curt was supposed to be mine. Levi took him away from me."

"Quit talking about how you want to fuck Curt Walsh, you dick." C.B. made a face. "I don't mind you being a queer, but don't throw it in my face, man."

Lucas didn't like that word and was about to say something when Rusty said his goodbyes and came back to their table. He looked up at Rusty's face when he slid into the booth.

"I know. I wanted to punch him too, but now is not the time. He didn't mean anything by it."

"The hell he didn't. I've heard that word enough to last me a lifetime. What's wrong with wanting to be with someone of the same sex? Not a damn thing, I tell you, and I wish people would get over their homophobic selves and let us live our lives however we see fit."

The waitress brought their food, giving him a wide-eyed look like she heard everything he said.

He wanted to punch something. "Let's eat and get the hell out of here before I say something to really get us in trouble." He ate the pie in front of him, but didn't really taste it as he shoveled it between his lips.

Rusty ate his cheeseburger, barely giving himself time to swallow before he took another bite. It was obvious they both figured it was best to get out before they said something they would regret later.

Within minutes, they were asking the waitress for the bill, throwing some money on the table, and leaving the diner behind.

They headed back to the hotel, although sex was the last thing on Lucas's mind now. Rusty probably still wanted to fuck again, but Lucas didn't. He wasn't sure why he let people like C.B. Parker get to him, but he did. Sentiment in their hometown seemed to be the same way and he knew his parents were homophobic too. If he even brought up the fact that he was gay to his parents or his brother, all hell would break loose. His sister, God love her, was supportive and happy for him. She kept asking when he might find someone special and settle down. He didn't know and it didn't look like it would be anytime soon. How could he? Settle down in Albuquerque with another guy? Yeah, that would go over like a lead balloon. People weren't accepting of the gay lifestyle in any sense of the word at home.

When Rusty opened the door to the hotel room, Lucas followed him inside, shutting the door behind them. Rusty eased himself down on the bed, leaving the chair by the window open for Lucas to settle himself in.

"I need a beer."

"There are still some left in the box. They might be a bit warm by now, but the ones in the refrigerator should be cold." Rusty slid his palms down the thighs of his jeans. Apparently, he was agitated for some reason. "Are you okay?"

"No, I'm not okay, Rusty. That comment bothered me to the point I'm so angry I could spit nails. I've heard that kind of shit my entire life and I know you have too. It pisses me off." Lucas opened the refrigerator, pulled out a beer, and popped the top. He drank almost half the can before he wiped his mouth with the back of his hand.

"I know."

"No you don't. I got bullied in high school if you remember correctly even though I didn't tell people I was gay. Some football players honed in on it somehow or they guessed. I'm not sure which, but it was hell living that life and keeping my sexuality a secret. I'm sure you felt the same way, although you weren't picked on by people at school. You had a steady girlfriend so you were able to show outwardly that you were straight. Why do you think I hate going home even during off season? I hate that town and the people in it. The only saving grace for me is the kids I teach. They don't care if I'm gay or straight. It doesn't matter to them as far as I know. They respect me for the teacher I am, not for my sexual preferences."

"Lucas, it doesn't matter what the other guys think or say. I don't care about them and you shouldn't either. They can label me anything they want. It's their problem, not ours."

"How can you say that? How can you be so calm about the whole thing? They aren't going to accept us the way we are, not in a million years, not on this circuit. What if the commission decides we can't ride bulls anymore because of who we are and who we want to be with? What then?"

"I don't know."

"I do. They can kiss my ass. I'll go ride somewhere else like Canada or something." Lucas drained the beer and grabbed another. He wanted to be numb, just for tonight, he needed it.

"Don't you think you've had enough alcohol?"

Lucas pointed one finger at Rusty, zeroing in on his face with the meanest glare he could muster. "Are you going to tell me what to do now too, Rusty, because if you are, I'll go back to my room with my beer and get shitfaced by myself."

"I don't think drinking is the answer, that's all."

"What is the answer?"

"I wish I knew, but I'm not afraid to show people I'm gay. I like being with men. If they can't accept that, then so be it. It's who I am."

"What were to happen if I came out as gay to the community and I lost my job? What if the circuit kicked us off because of it? What then? How would we make a living?"

"Move somewhere more accepting of the gay lifestyle, I guess."

"Like where? California?" He sucked down several gulps of the beer before stumbling back to the chair. "I can't live in that shit, Rusty. I need the buffalo grass, and the other things native to New Mexico. I was born and raised there."

"Then accept that everyone is not going to be as tolerable to our lifestyle as some. It comes with the territory of being gay, man. It's something we have to live with and fight for. The state has come a long way. Gays can even marry in New Mexico, unlike a few other states out there. We are progressing, but it will take time."

"I don't fucking want to wait for them to pull their heads out of their asses."

"We have to."

"You have to. I don't." He downed the rest of his beer, feeling the effects as his head swam a little from the alcohol. He probably should go back to his room. Sex was totally off the table tonight now that he was sitting here arguing with Rusty over stupid shit. Hell, it wasn't stupid shit, it was his life for crying out loud. What if the people in his subdivision ever found out he was gay? They could take it to the homeowners association, make his life miserable, and he might have to move or something. He didn't want to move. He liked his adobe style home with his small garden, his backyard pool, and his dog.

He glanced across the room at Rusty. What if someday he wanted a partner? What if he wanted someone to fall in love with, get married and raise a family? What if the neighborhood couldn't accept that kind of lifestyle from him? What then?

He needed to think.

After climbing to his feet, he dropped his empty can into the wastebasket, and headed for the door. The room was dark except for the small lamp they'd left on at the bedside, making it hard for him to find the door. He stubbed his foot on the dresser. "Fuck."

"What? Where are you going?"

"Back to my room. I'm done discussing this with you. You don't understand."

Rusty followed him a moment later. "Yes, I do, Lucas. I understand completely, but I'm not willing to let others rule my life, like you are."

"Fine. I'm letting others rule my life. So be it, but it is my life. I'll live it how I want to live it."

"By lying to yourself about who you are, what you want, and how you want to live? That's not living, that's existing and that's it."

"Then existing is what I'll do." He opened the door and stumbled out into the hall, banging his shoulder against the opposite wall. "Where's my room?"

"I don't know. You never told me."

He looked at Rusty standing in the doorway. "Oh, I remember. Six fourteen." He looked down the hall and then back at Rusty again. "Where's the elevator?"

"Well, for Christ's sake, I'll take you to your room. Let me grab my key."

Rusty disappeared inside for a minute while Lucas leaned against the wall, the whole thing spinning around like a merry-go-round. He hoped he wouldn't be sick. He didn't need that kind of thing happening in front of his lover. *Lover. Well, shit.* Yeah, they were lovers or at least the one time. What would happen when they got home tomorrow? Would they see each other again? Would Rusty come to his house? Would he go to Rusty's place now that he was living in his own home again since his leg was better? He didn't even know where Rusty lived.

When Rusty came back out the door, he shut it behind him before wrapping an arm around Lucas's waist. Lucas put an arm around Rusty's shoulder. "Thanks."

"For what?"

"Being my friend, even if I'm a dick."

"You aren't a dick. You're drunk."

"Yeah, I am, but I really mean it, Rusty. You're a good friend."

"Thanks."

"Sorry about not fucking tonight."

"We already did once. The rest can wait for another time."

"Will there be another time?"

"It's kind of up to you since you have a problem with people knowing about you. I kind of figured you wouldn't want me hanging around giving people any ideas, you know?"

They stumbled down the hallway toward the elevator. When they reached the doors, Rusty pushed the button. They had to go up two floors to reach his room.

Lucas felt bad. He'd really enjoyed doing Rusty's ass earlier and he'd been looking forward to Rusty's reciprocating, but he'd blown it by getting all stupid and drunk. Oh well, there would be other times, he hoped.

As the elevator opened, Rusty shoved him through the parted doors, and then pushed the button for the sixth floor. Now he remembered. His room was right near the elevator so as soon as Rusty got him near the door, he could send him on his way. He didn't want Rusty to come in his room because he might not be able to say no should Rusty decide he wanted to fuck anyway.

No, he would be strong. He didn't want to be the asshole in this situation even though he already felt bad.

"Rusty?"

"Yeah?"

"I'm sorry. I shouldn't have gotten drunk."

"It's okay."

"Thanks for helping me back to my room."

"Sleep it off, and I'll see you after we get home. My flight is early so I'll probably be gone before you get up."

He slid the keycard into the door lock. The door lock flashed green allowing them to open the door. "I can get it from here."

"Are you sure?"

"Yeah."

"Okay then. See you at home."

"Goodnight."

Chapter Four

Rusty peeled his gritty eyelids open at six a.m. to catch the early flight for home. Why the hell did he book a flight for so God awful early? The plane didn't leave until eight-thirty, but he needed to be there early. Vegas was a bear to get out of after finals, long lines, pissy people, and lots of pushing and shoving. Since his leg wasn't a hundred percent, he wanted to take his time walking to the gate. If he was way out there, it would be a while with his slow walk. He probably figured he wouldn't have slept the last night there with gambling and partying, but yeah, that didn't happen.

Home.

Why didn't he really look forward to going home today? His life wasn't bad. He had his small ranch with a few horses and cattle, a couple of ranch hands who helped him with the work. The ranch hands had basically kept the place running while he'd been laid up at his parent's place. Not that he didn't love his mom and dad, but that had been the worst couple of months of his life. The moment the cast had come off, he'd been back in his own home, living his own life.

He needed to get back to work, his work, bull riding. Practicing would have to be a priority if he was getting back on the circuit in January. He didn't have time to screw around.

Right now, he needed a shower, shave, and to put some clean clothes on. He'd packed most of his stuff last night after he ushered Lucas off to his room.

Lucas.

What the hell am I going to do about him?

Yeah, they'd fucked and it was great, but did he really want to get into a relationship with his friend on a steady basis?

After their *discussion* the night before, Lucas's words rang true for the most part. What would happen if they started dating on the circuit? Would it be acceptable? Did he even want that? Would the circuit even allow that kind of thing? It wasn't a publicized thing to be gay on the bull rider circuit even though he knew a few people who were. Levi Bond and Curt Walsh were rumored to be in a relationship and after Curt got hurt the other day in a bar fight, it appeared the relationship was on. Levi was at the arena for his rides and for what he had to be there for, but the rest of the time, he'd been at the local hospital.

Oh well, nothing he could do about it right now. He'd have plenty of time to think at home while they were on break.

He gingerly stood, grabbed his clean clothes, and headed for the bathroom. He didn't have time to waste lollygagging here in the hotel room. He had a flight to catch.

An hour later, found him walking the last few feet to the gate he needed to be at for his flight home. So far, he hadn't run into any fans although there were a few people who gave him the double take when they'd recognized him. Fans were what made bull riding all worthwhile. He loved interacting with the fans, especially the young boys who really idolized the riders.

Rusty slowly took a seat near the window, laying his carryon bag near his feet, and stretched out his legs as best he could. It would be thirty minutes or so before they bordered.

The waiting area was full of people.

Several were cowboys, a few he recognized, although he wasn't sure from where.

A young boy about twelve years old skidded to a halt in front of him. "Hey, aren't you Rusty Arnold?"

Rusty smiled. "Yes."

The kid produced a leather bull from behind his back. "Can you sign my bull?"

"Sure, buddy."

"You're the best rider there ever was."

"I wouldn't say that, but thanks."

"I think so. I'm sorry you got hurt. Are you going to ever ride again?"

"I plan to, yeah."

A thirty something young woman stopped next to the kid. "I'm sorry. When he saw you, he couldn't contain his excitement."

"It's okay. I love talking to fans."

"He's a huge fan of yours."

Rusty tipped his hat to the woman and smiled. "Thank you. I appreciate it."

"He was almost in tears when you got hurt a few months ago. How's the leg?"

"Doing fine. I should be back to riding soon."

"That's awesome."

"What's your name?"

"Jack."

Rusty dug out his sharpie marker and signed the bull in silver before handing it back to the kid. "There you go."

The kid beamed from ear to ear before his mother thanked him and ushered Jack back to his seat. Several other people stopped to say hi while they waited to board the plane, but most were respectful of his privacy.

Once he found his seat on the plane, he settled back, closed his eyes and tried to rest. It was a non-stop flight so it wouldn't take more than a couple of hours to get home, and man, he wanted to sleep in his own bed tonight. Hotels sucked.

His phone beeped with an incoming text message right before they were getting ready to shut the door, reminding him he needed to shut it off. He turned on the screen. The message was from Lucas.

Headed out. I hope you got some sleep. I didn't want to wake you this

morning. Sorry again about last night. See you
when I get home. Take
                              it easy.
                              Lucas

Rusty quickly sent a text back.

No problem. I'm on the plane getting ready to
push back. Be home in a
              couple of hours. Call me when you get in and we
can get together for a
                              beer.
                              Rusty

Rusty smiled as he powered down his phone for takeoff. At least Lucas was thinking about him as much as Rusty was thinking about Lucas. He really needed to decide what he wanted out of their relationship. Were they going to be occasional fuck buddies, just friends, or more?

An older gentleman sitting next to him asked, "Aren't you Rusty Arnold?"

"Yes, sir, I am."

"I've been following your career for some time, son. You're one of the best I've seen on the circuit."

"Thank you."

"Did you come out for finals?"

"Yes, sir. I wanted to watch even though I couldn't participate."

"It was a real disappointment when you got hurt."

"For me too. I was looking forward to the World Championship."

"A lot of people were rooting for you this year. Are you coming back?"

"I plan to, although I need to get my strength back in my legs from the break. It was a pretty bad one."

"I heard."

The engines roared as they took off, silencing the conversation between them for several minutes.

"It's going to be difficult to come back after being out for so long."

"I can do it. I'm sure of it."

The older man nodded in agreement. "How are you set for sponsors, Rusty?"

"I'm not sure, sir. I'd have to talk to my rep."

The man brought out his wallet and handed Rusty a business card. It read, Joseph R. Campbell, Rocking C Bucking Bulls and Beef Cattle.

Holy shit! This guy was the premium contractor for the circuit for bucking bulls. "Uh, thanks."

"I have a friend who is looking to sponsor a rider and I think you two would get along fantastic. He doesn't know much about bull riding, but he's looking to get into the ever expanding business of professional bull riders. I also know of another guy looking to sponsor a rider. He knows the business and is very experienced with the bulls. I'd like you to meet them both."

Rusty fingered the business card, wanting so badly to talk bulls with Mr. Campbell, but his tongue wouldn't form the words. He wanted to find out if he could practice on some of the bulls at The Rocking C to get back into shape since it wasn't far from his own place. "Sounds great." He realized the time to speak was now or he would lose his chance altogether. "Mr. Campbell?"

"Yes?"

"I need to ask a favor, but if you feel it wouldn't be fair or whatever, that's fine."

"What's that, son?"

"I need to get on some bulls in the next couple of months. Your place isn't far from mine. I have a practice barrel at the home place, but it's not quite the same as getting on real bulls. Your bulls are ranked some of the best on the circuit, and I could really use the time on the back of a few. Not your top ranking bulls, maybe just some up and coming ones or something."

"I don't know, Rusty. I don't want my bulls hurt in the off season."

"I know what you're saying. I would even be fine with using some younger bulls, not the best of the business. I just really need to get on some live bulls before I try to get back into the arena with them come January."

Mr. Campbell rubbed his chin for a moment. "You know, I think that would be a great idea. It would keep my bulls in shape so they don't get fat and lazy."

Rusty reached out to shake the man's hand. "You won't be sorry." When they clasped hands, Rusty was amazed at the firmness of Mr. Campbell's grip. He obviously worked his land right alongside his ranch hands.

"I'm sure I won't be, Rusty. You're an excellent rider. I would like to see you take the championship next year. Don't get me wrong, Levi did well and deserved it after his riding the last couple of months, but you were on top the whole year. You were headed for greatness and I want to see you obtain that this year."

"Thank you for the vote of confidence."

"You're more than welcome, son."

They made small talk about bulls, the circuit, cattle, and ranch life for the rest of the trip home.

After the plane landed, Rusty made his way down the walkway toward the door. The flight attendant shook his hand and told him to get well soon so they could see him ride again. He was humbled that so many people were rooting for him to be back on the circuit. It was amazing to know he had so many fans that had been torn up when he got hurt.

By the time he made his way down to the carousel to retrieve his bag, it was the last one going around on the conveyor belt. He grinned and shook his head before grabbed the rolling suitcase so he could head out to his truck.

His leg ached as he limped slowly out to the parking area, making him wonder if he'd be ready to ride again in January or ever. He certainly didn't want to go out permanently with an injury like this. He still had a few good years ahead of him before he planned to retire.

Sweat poured down his temple as he approached his truck. He was out of breath and really hurting when he slung his suitcase into the back, climbed into the cab, and shut the door. He had to rest his head on the steering wheel as he willed the pain to go away, his heart rate to come back to normal, and his breathing to slow down.

A few minutes later, he backed out of the parking spot before heading out toward the toll booth. Once he paid his parking ticket, he drove out the exit headed for the interstate and home.

He drove down the gravel drive leading to his house about forty-five minutes later. The light blue ranch style home with white trim, big windows, and long porch was his favorite part of living where he did. The big barn behind the house was his pride and joy. He loved raising the animals he had and it was all bought and paid for. He didn't have to worry about the bank taking it away or anything. Riding bulls had been good to him in that way. Even if he had to retire right now, he could make it just fine with what he had in the bank.

As he popped the door to the truck open and slid out, he stumbled a bit on his stiff leg before grabbing his suitcase out of the rear of the extended cab, and shutting the door behind him.

His foreman came out of the barn wiping his hands on a towel. "Hey, Rusty. How was the trip?"

"Hey, Nick. The trip was good. I'm beat though." He rubbed his aching thigh. "I think I pushed too much." He shook Nick's hand. "I'm glad to be home."

"I'm sure."

"How are things around here?"

"Good. Nothing much going on." Nick held up the towel. "I'm working on the old truck. It broke down again on us a couple of days ago."

"We need to get rid of it and buy a new one."

Nick stuffed the rag in his back pocket. "Yeah, but it's a classic, Rusty. They don't make them like that anymore."

"I know."

"How's the leg?"

"Not very good right now. I'm in a lot of pain."

"Well, you'd better get inside and rest then. You need to be in top condition to get back into the race next year."

"I know." Rusty started for the house. "Oh, you'll never guess who I sat next to on the plane from Vegas?"

"Who?"

"Joseph Campbell of the Rocking C Bucking Bulls."

"Holy shit, really? He's like famous."

"At least on the circuit, yeah. His bulls are busting their way through the ranks. Mr. Tough belongs to him and so does Lucifer's Chaos."

"Aren't those the two who Levi had to ride for the championship?"

"Lucifer's Chaos was the winning ride."

"Damn. That's one rank bull."

"Levi made it look easy though. I take it you were watching?"

"Hell yeah, I was watching. My boss is a bull rider. I watch every week."

Rusty laughed. He really liked Nick, not in the sexual kind of way, but he liked him as a friend, a good friend. Besides, he knew for a fact that Nick was straight as a piece of fence railing and Nick knew Rusty was gay.

"I'd better get inside and get off this leg. Are you coming up for supper?"

"Nah. I have a date."

"Who is she? Someone I know?" Rusty asked, taking the weight off his bad leg as he leaned on the truck. He really needed to get inside instead of making small talk.

"No, she's new in town. Works at the diner. Her name is Marie."

"You'll have to introduce me sometime."

"And risk you taking her away from me? Not on your life, Rusty."

They laughed together as Rusty pushed himself off the truck. "I'm going inside. I'll catch you tomorrow probably. My bed is calling my name early this evening, but I've got some work to do on the books this afternoon."

"Take it easy. I'll be around until five if you need something. You know, just holler."

"Will do. Thanks, Nick." Rusty made his way to the porch. The two steps going up seemed like a mountain right now with the pain in his thigh. He took a couple of long slow breaths, hoisted his good leg up on the step and dragged his stiff one up behind it. He had a long way to go before he would be able to ride again, at this rate. He needed to talk to his doctor and find out if things were as they should be so he could get on the practice barrel next week.

He hobbled into the house, down the hall, and into his office, before easing himself down in his leather office chair with a heavy sigh. *Pain pill. Damn, I should have grabbed one before I left my suitcase in the hall.* He pushed himself to his feet to work his way back to where he left his duffle bag. If his mom knew he was in this much pain, she'd be over to his house in a heartbeat.

"Well, she's not going to find out."

After he managed to retrieve his pain pills and a bottle of water he'd purchased at the airport, he slowly worked his way back to his office. He needed to look at the books today since he had a load of feed coming next week and some cattle to sell off the following week.

As he took the pressure off his leg by sliding down into the chair, he exhaled on a rush of relief. Opening the drawer to his left, he took out the receipts Nick had left for him while he was gone. The computer to his right booted up with a push of a button. He really hated doing the paperwork required of ranch work, but at least his place was profitable.

For the next several hours, he worked on all the stuff he'd neglected while he was off in Vegas. By the time he was done, the sun had long set outside and his stomach growled from not eating. He flicked off the computer and the lamp on his desk before he pushed himself to his feet, relieved to have some of the pain gone in his leg. As he made his way to the kitchen, he hoped there was something to eat since he hadn't had a chance to get any food before he came home. *Maybe I'll order a pizza.*

His cell phone jingled in his pocket. When he pulled it out, he smiled a little when he realized it was Lucas. "Hey," he said, after he put the phone to his ear. "Are you home?"

"Yeah, just pulled in and I'm beat. I hate these long drives."

"Part of riding the circuit."

"Yeah, I know. I've probably put a hundred thousand miles on this beast in the last two years with all the back and forth from coast to coast."

"Me too."

"We should start traveling together. Save on gas and wear on the vehicles since we live in the same town."

"We can talk about it, sure."

"Is everything okay? You aren't still pissed about last night, are you?"

"I wasn't pissed in the first place, Lucas."

"I would have been."

"Why? You were stating your opinion on how you see your life. You are welcome to think how you want to. I'm just not sure I agree with you."

Lucas grunted into the phone. Rusty smiled to himself. He'd come to realize after being around Lucas a bit that his friend tended to pout when things didn't go his way.

"Are you up for a beer tonight?"

"No. I'm really hurting. I'm going to take another pain pill after I eat and hit the bed."

"Okay."

"Sorry."

"It's fine. I'm pretty tired myself. I need to get my dog from my parent's place. Poor thing doesn't know who I am half the time since I'm hardly home. I do bring him home when I'm out on breaks in the season though."

"That's why I don't have a dog or cat. I only have farm animals who can be taken care of by the guys on my place."

"You know, I don't even know where you live."

"Out off of Highway 314, south of town."

"Oh. Do you have property?"

"Yeah, two hundred acres. I'm kind of out here by myself."

"That must be nice."

"It is. I don't have to deal with my parents coming out here pushing me to take over their place. Russell can do it." Rusty pulled the menu off the refrigerator to dial for pizza as soon as he was off the phone with Lucas. His stomach rumbled again.

"I'll let you go. It sounds like you are getting something to eat."

"Yeah, I'm going to order pizza."

"Sounds good. I…uh…I'll talk to you later then."

"Okay. Goodnight."

"Night."

Rusty hung up the phone and shook his head. *If that wasn't the most awkward conversation two friends can have, I don't know what is.* He dialed the pizza place, gave them his order, and then hung up. It would be thirty minutes before they could get it to him, but it would be worth it in the end.

He grabbed a beer out of the ice box, popped the top, and lifted it to his lips. Luckily, he'd had a few left over in the refrigerator from before he went to Vegas. The beer slid down his throat in a cooling wash, taking away the worries of the day with it. He'd only have one since it wasn't a good idea to drink and take pain pills together, but man, it tasted good.

He probably should call his parents and let them know he was home. *Nah. I'll call tomorrow. I don't want a lecture tonight.* He took a seat on the leather couch, grabbed the remote and flipped on the television to CBS sports. They would be rerunning the finals on that channel and he'd like to see some of the rides up close. It helped him to be a better rider himself if he could analyze what the others did. He had every event on DVD and watched them religiously, especially his own rides.

After his pizza arrived, he settled back on the couch to watch as he ate.

When Lucas's ride came on, he sat forward in his seat, watching his friend wrap his hand with precision. The moment he nodded for them to open the gate, Rusty held his breath. He knew how the ride came out, he'd been in the audience when it had happened, but watching it with the camera right on the rider, was even better. Lucas made the ride look fluid and effortless.

The bull came out of the chute bucking solid, spinning into Lucas's riding hand before switching it up and turning back to the other side. The animal was almost vertical at one point, with his hind legs bucking so hard and his front feet planted on the ground, Lucas's back almost rested on the bull's haunches.

When the buzzer sounded, Rusty released the breath he'd been holding as Lucas jumped free. The ride was text book and one Rusty knew Lucas scored well on. It was enough to put him in the top ten of the standings, but not enough to get him some real points on the leader.

The finals were tough. It was the best of the best on the circuit. Staying on wasn't enough. You needed to score in the high eighties or low nineties on every ride.

Levi came up next.

Rusty watched with avid attention. He knew Levi won the World Champion buckle, but to be able to watch the ride showed him exactly why Levi had won. The man was brilliant on the back of a bull. He would be tough to beat next year. Rusty knew he had his work cut out for him.

As the evening wore on, Rusty got sleepy as the pain pills he'd taken earlier began to kick in. He needed to make his way to his bedroom, strip down to his skivvies, and sleep for about eight hours.

By the time he made it to the bedroom, he was almost stumbling. The pills sure kicked his ass when he took them, that was another reason he needed to get off them. It wouldn't do any good to get hooked on them and need them all the time to function. He found the bottle next to the bed, lifted it to look through the yellow plastic, and then shook it. He didn't have many left. He would have to get the doctor to prescribe more. The pain was difficult to deal with without the medication. There'd been a cowboy or two on the circuit who had been hooked on pain pills after an injury.

He'd be all right. He could handle them. Besides, he only took them when he needed them.

Once he stripped down to his underwear, he pushed the covers back on the bed, slid beneath the cold sheets, and then covered up.

Moonlight fell across the bed in a wash of silver through the gauzy curtains on the window. A cool breeze lifted the panels in a slow sway of material, bringing the air to him where he laid. He loved sleeping with the window open even in the winter. Snuggling down under the covers with the room temperature almost freezing, he could sleep like a baby.

He slowly closed his eyes, letting his mind wander.

A work roughed hand smoothed down his chest, taking the sheet with it as it continued down to the point where his cock stood long and hard, against his stomach.

When he glanced to his right, Lucas's blue eyes sparkled in the moonlight.

"Miss me?"

"Hell yeah. Where have you been? I've been waiting for you to come to me."

"I wasn't sure you still wanted me."

"Why wouldn't I? I've been hard since the last time we fucked."

"I screwed up, Rusty. We argued. I don't like arguing with you. You're my friend."

"We are more than friends, Lucas, lest you've forgotten."

"How could I forget? Being buried in your tight ass made my whole trip to Vegas worth every painful minute on the back of those bulls."

"Enough talk. Suck me."

Lucas pushed the remainder of the sheet past his hips moments before his warm mouth closed over the head of his cock. A moan escaped from his lips, the sound coming deep from within his throat.

The slick tongue encircled the head of his cock, around and around as one hand gripped his shaft in a steel fist. Suction from the mouth pulling on the end of his dick brought his ass off the bed.

"Easy, my friend. I want to give you pleasure."

"You're driving me insane." He pumped his hips a few times, dragging the head of his cock along the rough pad of Lucas's tongue. "I'm going to die from pleasure."

Lucas moved down to Rusty's balls, sucking one nugget into his mouth before he mumbled, "What a way to go."

Rusty pushed against Lucas's shoulder hard enough to shove him off and onto his back. "Enough. My turn to torture you."

The moment Lucas lay sprawled out like a gift to the gods, Rusty swooped in, taking his cock into his mouth clear to the back of his throat.

"Uhhnnn."

The sound escaping Lucas's throat brought a shot of pleasure straight to Rusty's cock. He'd done that for his lover—brought him to pleasure so quickly he was unable to make a coherent sound.

Rusty pleasured Lucas with his tongue and mouth for several minutes, sucking, licking, stroking, and playing until the other man was begging for Rusty to take him quickly.

When Rusty backed off and looked down at Lucas's cock, the purple veiny member almost looked painfully hard. He knew that kind of pain as his own cock strained against his stomach in an excruciatingly solid state. "Roll over and spread those cheeks."

Lucas rolled onto his stomach as Rusty reached for the lube in his nightstand drawer. He positioned himself behind Lucas as he dribbled the wet liquid down the crack of his ass before rubbing some into the tissues. "Are you ready for me?"

"Hell yeah." He groaned as he laid his forehead against the pillow on the bed. "Hurry."

Rusty slowly pushed his cock through the ring of muscles in Lucas's ass, shuddering like a leaf in a windstorm as he penetrated deeply. "Ah, fuck."

"Move. God, please, move."

With a snap of his hips, Rusty drove his cock the rest of the way into Lucas's ass until his pelvis met the rounded flesh of his butt cheeks. "You feel fantastic."

"Fuck me. Please. I need this so bad."

"Me too, lover, me too." Rusty slowly removed his cock until it was almost free before shoving it back in. The sensation was spectacular. The smooth walls of the channel surrounding him felt incredible. He shivered at the sensations bombarding him while he continued to slowly stroke his cock in and out of Lucas's ass.

His cock got explicably harder as his balls drew up in preparation for his orgasm. He couldn't hold back much longer, but he wanted Lucas to come with him.

He reached around to stroke his lover's cock. "Come for me, Lucas, come hard."

Lucas exploded in a gut wrenching orgasm that coated Rusty's hand with his cum as Rusty pounded into Lucas's flesh until he too lost control of his pleasure and came hard.

Rusty came awake with a start, his cock hard and aching with unsatisfied lust for the man who wasn't really there. He shoved his hand through his hair, cussing a blue streak at the throbbing in his balls. "I need a cold shower."

He moved his legs over the side of the bed and got to his feet to head to the bathroom. *What I wouldn't give to have Lucas here right now.*

A knock sounded on his front door as he made his way past the end of his bed.

He glanced at the clock. Midnight. *Who in the hell could that be at this hour?*

Chapter Five

Lucas stood at Rusty's door, swaying a bit from too much alcohol. He'd hit the bar when he'd got in, needing to reduce the stress driving from Vegas had put on his body. His joints were stiff and sore after sitting in the truck for nine hours.

He knocked again before glancing at his watch. *Shit. Midnight.* Was Rusty even awake?

The porch light clicked on.

Apparently so.

"Whose there?"

"It's me, Lucas."

The door opened to reveal Rusty, all dark five-foot-eleven inches of him, standing in nothing but a pair of sweat pants.

"What are you doing here? It's midnight for crying out loud."

"I know."

"Wow." Rusty waved his hand in front of his face. "What bar were you at?"

"The Rusty Nail." He put his hand on the doorframe. "I had a few."

"Apparently." Rusty propped his hand up high on the edge of the door.

Lucas swayed on his feet. "I'm horny."

"Yeah?"

"Yep. I need you to fuck me."

"You need to be sober if I'm going to fuck you, my friend."

"Aw, hell, Rusty. My dick is so hard, I could pound nails with it. Please?"

"No way, mister. I don't fuck drunk guys. I want you to remember me pounding your ass until you come so hard, you see stars."

"Well shit." He opened the screen. "Can I sleep on your couch, man? I shouldn't be driving."

Rusty didn't look convinced. "You drove out here like that?"

"Yes. I wanted to see you."

"You idiot."

Rusty grabbed him by the shirt front, yanked him up hard against his chest, and slammed his mouth down against Lucas's. He darted his tongue between Lucas's lips, dragging a groan from deep inside his chest as he returned the kiss. Their tongues dueled as Lucas grabbed Rusty's cock in his palm through his pants. The hard flesh of Rusty's cock had him moaning around Rusty's tongue.

Their breaths mingled as Rusty's backed off. "I won't fuck you tonight, but rest assured, your ass is mine come morning."

Lucas whimpered quietly, hoping Rusty didn't hear the need in his voice. He knew Rusty was right, but it didn't make his cock less achy. "Fine. Point me in the direction of the couch so I can sleep off this buzz."

Rusty backed up, leaving the doorway open for Lucas to move past him. The scent Rusty had on drove Lucas wild with desire. He wanted to bury his nose in Rusty's neck, biting his way to the man's nipples in long strokes of his tongue and teeth. *God, I'm horny.*

"Are you sure we can't fuck?"

"Nope, not tonight," Rusty said, shutting the door behind him as he made his way inside.

"Well hell." Lucas flopped down on the couch, his arm over his eyes. "You know, this is wrong, right? I wanted you to ream my ass."

"I know."

"I could have found someone at the bar to go home with."

"Probably, but you didn't."

"No, I didn't."

"Was there a reason for that?"

"I wanted you."

"Nice to know." Rusty's voice came from farther away. "Goodnight."

Lucas grunted in response. His dick hurt. His stomach churned. His eyelids felt heavy. Maybe Rusty was right, he wouldn't have wanted to miss remembering Rusty in his ass for the world.

Sunlight streamed through the window on the front of the house, making Lucas's head hurt as he opened his eyes.

He smelled coffee and something else—food.

After he slowly sat up, his head in his hands, he realized the smell of coffee was coming from a steaming cup held under his nose.

"Black or cream and sugar?"

He reached for the cup, taking it between his shaking hands and sipping the nectar of the gods. "Black." He took another sip. "Thank you. You're a godsend."

"I figured you might be a bit hungover."

"A bit, yeah."

"How's the head?"

He peered up at his friend through squinty eyes. "Feels like someone is piercing it with a jackhammer and none too lightly either."

"How's your stomach?"

"About to eat itself."

"I'll get you some Alka-Seltzer."

"Yes, please."

Rusty came back a few minutes later with a cup of water that bubbled like it was alive.

After Lucas set his cup on the coffee table, he took the glass from Rusty's hand, downing the awful tasting liquid in a few gulps. He knew it would help if he didn't die from the taste first. "Good grief, that stuff is bad."

"Yes, but it will help you in the long run if you don't throw it up first." Rusty made his way back into the kitchen off to the left while Lucas laid back on the couch, his arm over his eyes to keep the sunlight from stabbing through his eyelids like an icepick. This would teach him to drink too much. Yeah, probably not. He'd been in a state when he'd hit home turf last evening, wishing he'd been with Rusty. He wanted his friend—badly and when he'd been approached at the club by several men, he'd realized how much he didn't want them. The Rusty Nail was a known gay bar in Albuquerque, one he frequented often when he wanted a hook up, but this time he turned the other men down one after another.

It had been really stupid of him to drive to Rusty's at midnight, drunk as he was, but leave it to his friend to take care of him by making him stay the night, even if it was with a promise of hot sex come morning. Of course, Lucas realized sex was probably off the table until his head and stomach felt better.

"Ready for food?"

"Yeah." Lucas threw his legs over the side of the couch, climbed to his feet, and wobbled a bit as he got his bearings. His head didn't pound quite as much as it had even a few minutes before. He made his way into the kitchen and took a seat at the kitchen table with the large leaf. The thing could sit twelve people easy. Lucas realized Rusty probably had his ranch hands eating with him normally. "How many guys do you have working here?"

"Ten right now, including the foreman."

"They aren't eating this morning?"

"It's their day off. They usually eat in town on Saturday mornings since they party hard on Friday night."

"Oh."

Rusty slid some bacon, eggs, and a couple of biscuits in front of him as his stomach rumbled. Apparently, it had decided it was hungry now.

When Rusty took the chair across from him, he let his gaze wander over his friend's face. He looked kind of haggard and drawn. His eyes looked bloodshot, his face looked pale, and he had bags under his eyes. "You okay?"

"Yeah, why?"

"You look like shit." Lucas shoved a bite of eggs between his lips before taking a bite of a piece of bacon. He'd never eaten anything so delicious, he decided. Rusty was a damned good cook. "This is excellent."

Rusty glanced down at his plate, took a tentative bite, and then pushed it away.

"You aren't eating?"

"I'm not really hungry."

"You need to eat, Rusty."

"I know. I'm just not hungry."

"Are you still taking those pain pills?"

Rusty brought his gaze up to his before he looked back down. "No. I quit taking them."

"When was the last time you took some? Maybe you need to take one. You look like you're hurting."

Rusty's gaze came up again and then went back to his plate as he picked up the piece of bacon, bringing it to his lips. "It's been a couple of days. I can do without them."

Lucas got the impression Rusty wasn't being honest with him. He'd seen him take several in Vegas when they were together, and he knew his friend still hurt pretty badly from the broken leg, although he didn't seem to be limping on it as much. "Are you in a lot of pain?"

Rusty banged his hand on the table. "I'm fine, Lucas. Let it go."

"All right, buddy. I don't mean to pry." Lucas held up his hands in a defensive posture.

"Well, you are." Rusty climbed to his feet and dumped the plate in the sink. "I need to check on Nick." He waved his hand toward Lucas's plate. "Finish your breakfast. I'll be right back."

Lucas watched as Rusty slowly made his way to the front door, a slight limp to his gait, and a grimace on his face. His friend was in a lot of pain if he knew anything, and he couldn't figure out why he didn't want to take the pain pills the doctor had given him, if he was hurting that much.

When he finished his food, he put what was left of Rusty's down the garbage disposal, rinsed both plates and put them in the dishwasher. It was the least he could do since his friend had made breakfast.

He grabbed another cup of coffee from the pot and leaned against the counter, his thoughts in turmoil. Why had he been so desperate to see Rusty the night before? Why hadn't he just hooked up with one of the men at the bar like he normally would have? Seems his cock had other ideas. Oh well. He'd get his rocks off where he could and then move on with his life, his career in bull riding, and worry about the rest later. Relationships weren't his thing. Not now, not ever. He figured he didn't have time for someone exclusive in his life. Not with his career taking off. He'd done well this year with bull riding, bringing in a good bit of money from his wins on the circuit. Money wouldn't be a problem for a bit for him, of that he could be sure. The balance in his checking account confirmed that. Since he didn't have a lot of bills, he could relax until the next season started.

New York would be here before he knew it. The whole crazy life of riding, traveling, schmoozing the fans, and working the crowd would start over for another nine months. It was the life he'd chosen.

He took sip of the hot liquid, burning his tongue in the process. "Ouch."

The screen banged shut.

Lucas turned around to come face to face with a man he thought he'd never see again.

"Hi, Lucas."

"Nick." *Holy shit.* Now what the hell was he going to do? "What are you doing here?"

"I'm Rusty's foreman."

He shoved his hands through his hair. He never thought he'd ever see the guy who was his first gay sexual encounter and the one he thought he'd fallen in love with. He'd met Nick at The Rusty Nail several years ago, when he'd first went out to find a gay lover. He'd always known about his sexual preferences, but when he couldn't bring himself to go after Rusty, he needed to move on and find someone else. Nick had been there that night and when Lucas had managed to get pretty drunk, he'd been the one to take Lucas home. Nick hadn't been working for Rusty back then, he'd just been a ranch hand working the local places during the heavy work seasons.

"What are *you* doing here, Lucas?"

"Rusty and I have always been friends. I got pretty drunk last night and came over here. Rusty let me sleep on his couch. We ride the circuit together, so yeah, we know each other. You knew that."

"I didn't know you were that close."

Lucas raked his hand down his face and then across his mouth. "We've known each other a long time. We used to ride bulls in high school together." He took a sip of his coffee to hide his shaking hands.

Nick moved toward the coffee pot to pour himself a cup. Lucas took a seat, his legs feeling a bit weak at this point.

The older man sipped his coffee as he leaned against the countertop, eyeing Lucas over the rim of his cup.

Lucas wasn't sure what to say. What did you say to the man you thought you loved, but who'd walked away the moment the words had passed your lips? *I hate what you made me become. I hate that you broke my heart. I hate you for who you are.* "What do you want, Nick?"

"Nothin', Lucas. I'm just getting a cup of coffee before I start my day." Nick lifted the cup, silently saluting him with it before he took another sip.

"Bullshit. I'm sure you saw my truck outside."

"How did I know it was your truck?" Nick didn't move. "You are making this into way more than it needs to be, friend."

"You're the one who walked away."

"You were getting too serious. I didn't want serious, still don't. I'm good the way I am."

The door behind him banged shut. When he turned around, he wasn't surprised to see Rusty standing in the doorway.

"What's going on?"

"Nothing," Nick said, drinking the last of his coffee before putting the cup in the sink. "I'm heading out, boss. The guys are in the south pasture. Since that mare foaled last night, I'll be out riding fence for the day." Nick tipped his hat as he walked past Lucas. "See you, Lucas."

Rusty's gaze never left his face. *Fuck it! It's not like we are in a relationship or anything. We are fuck buddies, nothing more. I'm done with relationships.* Nick had it right. He didn't want anything serious, now or ever, especially in this bigoted town. "I guess I should be getting home."

"Oh?"

"Yeah. Sorry to take up your couch like that, but thanks for letting my crash here."

Rusty walked into the kitchen, grabbed a cup of coffee, and then took a seat at the table. "You want to tell me what that was all about?"

"What?"

Rusty tipped his head to the side, studying Lucas's face. "I'm not stupid, Lucas. You apparently have some history with Nick."

Lucas didn't know how much to reveal. It really didn't matter what his relationship with Nick was or it shouldn't matter to Rusty. "It's nothing."

"It didn't look like nothing."

Lucas sighed. "Nick and I were lovers at one time. I thought I was in love with him. He wasn't in love with me. He walked away."

"Oh."

"See. It was nothing." Lucas climbed to his feet and put his coffee cup in the sink. "I'd better go."

"If you want to."

"I think it's best."

"Sure."

* * * *

Rusty watched Lucas walk out the door wondering what the hell just happened. *Lucas and Nick? Wow.* Thoughts ran jumbled across his brain as he tried to imagine his foreman with Lucas. He wanted to know when, where, why, and how the relationship came about. This was the first he'd heard of it so they must have kept it on the quiet side. That wouldn't surprise him though since Lucas thought the whole town hated anyone who was gay.

The coffee scorched his tongue when he took another sip. Lucas had given him a clue as to a past relationship that had gone sour, but then again, he hadn't talked about his past much either.

It's not like they were going for something permanent where they needed to talk about these things, right?

His heart did a little squeeze.

Okay, maybe Lucas wasn't going for anything permanent, but Rusty kind of wanted to find someone to spend his life with and the thought of that being Lucas wasn't an unpleasant one. If he could only convince his friend they might be good together on a forever kind of basis.

Whoa. Wait a minute. What the hell am I thinking? We've fucked once. I can't get my balls in a bunch about someone I've slept with once.

Rusty continued to sip his coffee as he contemplated what he wanted from his so called relationship with Lucas. Yes, they were or had slept together. He'd intended to do it again this morning, but after the scene with Nick, he got the feeling Lucas was a bit preoccupied.

Jealousy sliced through him when he thought about Nick and Lucas together.

How can I be jealous?

"This is a bit crazy." He finished off his coffee before getting to his feet. "And what's this shit about Nick being gay anyway? When did that happen? He's worked for me for years and I didn't know he was gay!"

A soft knock sounded on the screen door as Rusty set his cup in the sink. He had work to do and these constant interruptions weren't helping. When he turned to see who was there, he was surprised to see his twin. "Russell? To what do I owe this surprise visit?"

"I need to ask you for a favor," he said, opening the screen.

Rusty felt his left eyebrow go up in a questioning expression. Russell never asked him for anything if he didn't have to. "What's that?"

"I hurt myself the other day at the ranch. Twisted by ankle a little. It's swollen and bruised, but I don't want to go to the doctor. You know I don't have insurance. Can I get a couple of your pain pills from you to tie me over for a few days?"

"I suppose. I don't have very many. I need to get another refill from the doctor soon myself."

"Be careful. Those things are addicting."

"I know that. I only use them sparingly and when I'm really hurting. Today is a good day. I might even go out and ride the barrel a bit. You know, get some rhythm."

"Yeah, yeah, where are they, in your room?"

"Yeah, I'll get them."

Russell moved past him in a hurry. "It's fine. I'll go. You shouldn't be doing too much with that leg."

Rusty tipped his head to the side as he watched his twin scurry up the hall to his bedroom. "They are on the nightstand."

"Got it!"

A minute later he came back. "You're right. You don't have very many of them. You should call the doctor today. You probably need to get seen anyway, right? You've had the cast off a couple of weeks, but I know it takes a while for a break like that to heal."

"Yeah, they say six months. I hope it's better soon. I only have a few months to get back into riding shape."

"I'm sure." He walked past Rusty, headed for the door. "Thanks, bro."

As the screen banged against the frame, Rusty shrugged and walked out onto the porch a moment behind his brother. A large dust cloud followed his brother's truck down the driveway, obscuring the back of the vehicle in dirt.

He wanted to get the barrel setup and work on his motions today while the sun was shining, and the weather wasn't too warm. It usually stayed in the seventies in October and the first part of November, but during the summer the barn would be stifling hot. When he stepped out on the porch a nice breeze lifted a bit of his hair from the nape of his neck. He pulled his hat lower on his forehead to keep it from flying off as he slowly took the steps down to the ground in front of the porch.

Nick had ridden off earlier, so he was alone on the ranch. He needed someone to work with him before he could get on the barrel. It required an operator to make the motions of the bull while he *rode* the thing. He could call Lucas, he guessed, but after the way his lover left this morning, he wasn't too sure he'd want to come back even though they both could use the practice.

He pulled out his wallet, opening it and removing the card he'd been given on the airplane. Maybe he should call Mr. Campbell and see if he could go over there. Wait! What about the bull riding school that opened out near Los Lunas put on by an upstart who wanted to get into the bucking bulls business like Mr. Campbell. The guy was a former pro rodeo rider who'd retired after several years riding bulls. What did he call the school? Surely they had a practice barrel he might be able to use today.

Rusty turned on his heel and headed back inside the house. He probably would have to check the Internet since bull riding schools, especially new ones, weren't listed in the phone book.

The cooler interior of the house washed over him as he stepped through the doorway and walked past the back of the couch, heading for his office. It shouldn't be too hard to find them on the computer.

After he took a seat behind his desk, he turned on his computer, pulled up the web, and typed in bull riding schools, Albuquerque, New Mexico. Sure enough, his search located the Double L Ranch and Bull Riding School. He jotted down the number before picking up his cell phone and dialing.

"Double L Ranch and Bull Riding School, how can I help you?"

"Hi there. My name is Rusty Arnold and I wanted to know if there was any way I could get some practice time on a barrel today? Do you have one I could use?"

"The Rusty Arnold? The guy who rides the pro circuit?"

"Uh, yes, ma'am."

"Wow."

Silence filled the line for a moment.

"Do you have a barrel I could use for today? I have one on my place, but I don't have anyone around to help me. I need some practice. You see, I got stepped on a few months ago and—"

"I know. I saw your ride. I'm sorry you were hurt."

"Thank you, but can you help me?"

"Sure thing, Mr. Arnold. Do you know where we are located?"

"Los Lunas off Highway 314, right?"

"Yes, sir."

The women rattled off some directions to him that he jotted down on a piece of paper. "Thank you. I will see you in about thirty to forty-five minutes."

"Wonderful. See you soon."

Once he hung up the phone, he got to his feet and headed for his bedroom. He needed to change into some comfortable clothes and slip on his boots and hat before grabbing his gear bag with his bull rope in it. He probably didn't need his chaps, but he kind of felt naked without them, so he figured he'd take them anyway.

When he reached his room, he started to gather the things he would need, debating on whether he should take a pain pill with him to take right before he came home. *Probably not a good idea. I won't want to be driving with that stuff in my system. I can wait until I get back here, I guess.* He glanced at his nightstand where the bottle of pills sat.

Empty.

"What the hell?"

Chapter Six

Russell took my entire bottle of pills. There had to be at least twenty in there. Rusty thrust his fingers through his hair before grabbing his cell phone and dialing his brother. "Russell?

"Yeah?"

"What the hell, man. You took all of my pills."

"No, I didn't. I only took what was left which was only about a hand full. I need them Rusty. You don't understand."

"I understand this, you don't need them that much. If you need pain pills because you hurt yourself, go to the damn doctor. It doesn't cost that much. Mom and Dad would probably pay for it anyway."

"You are such an ass."

"Bring them back."

"I can't."

"Why?"

Hesitation crackled through the phone line before Russell finally said, "I took them already."

"You're lying. If you took a handful, you had to have taken about ten of them. Why would you take ten pills at once?"

"Okay. I have a few left."

"Then bring them back."

"I can't. I'm busy, Rusty. Some of us work for a living, you know."

"You're an asshole. Now I have to go to town to get a refill from the pharmacy before I can go do some practicing."

"You can get more?"

"Yes, but you can forget getting anymore from me. If you need something, go to the doctor and get a prescription yourself."

"Kiss my ass, brother. I'm so fucking done with you, it's not funny. You're all about *the* Rusty Arnold, you can't see your way to helping your own family. I wish you weren't my brother."

Russell disconnected the call, leaving Rusty to stare at the phone in confusion. *What the hell just happened?*

Rusty shook his head as he set the phone down on the comforter to gather the stuff he needed in his duffle bag. Thoughts of his family kept bouncing through his brain. Something wasn't right with Russell, and he needed to find out what it was. After all, Russell was his twin and what affected him had always affected Rusty on some visceral level.

The moment he was ready, he grabbed his phone again, picked up the empty bottle of pills and called in his refill. He could pick them up on his way back from the Double L, he figured, giving them enough time to fill it before he came to pick it up.

With a sigh, he grabbed his bag and headed slowly down the hall toward the front of the house. He hoped he wasn't rushing the riding thing, but he needed to get back into shape, otherwise he wouldn't be able to compete in January.

Thirty minutes later, he pulled up to the big gates of the Double L and drove down the long, gravel driveway toward the large barn in the distance. A huge two story southern plantation type house sat off the left. He whistled softly at the big structure as he drove on past and parked in front of the barn.

A moment later, a pretty dark-haired girl came trotting out through a door situated in the side of the barn. As she reached the side of his truck, he opened the door.

"Hi, Rusty."

"Hello."

"I'm Shelly. My parents own the place. I talked to you on the phone."

"It's nice to meet you."

"You too." She rocked back on her heels as she stuffed her hands in the front of a very short pair of shorts. "Wow. I never thought I'd get to meet you. You're even cuter in person."

He smiled. "Thanks."

She waved one hand. "Sorry. Listen to me flirting with you." She turned on her booted heel and moved a couple of steps away before she glanced back over her shoulder. "Follow me. Dad is waiting inside. When he heard you were coming, he got all excited. I hope you don't mind, but he had a class already scheduled, so there are a few students around. They are excited to meet you, too."

Although the thought of potential fans watching him kind of put him off, he figured it was the price he needed to pay since it wasn't costing him much to use their facilities. When he walked into the barn, he was floored to see more than thirty people standing around. A small round of applause surprised him and made him blush.

A tall, portly man with a straw cowboy hat approached with his hand out. "Rusty Arnold. Good to see you out and about, young man. My name is Logan Tyler, owner of the Double L."

"It's nice to meet you, Mr. Tyler."

"Call me Logan." He pumped Rusty's hand several times. "I hear you need some barrel time?"

"Yes, sir. Since my accident I haven't had a chance to do any riding, and I thought using the barrel might be okay before I actually get on a bull."

"Well, son, I have both and you are certainly welcome to use either one."

"I appreciate that, Logan." He glanced at the group of boys ranging from thirteen to eighteen as they stood around the barrel, some sitting on the fencing nearby, and some sitting in the stands on the other side. "You've got quite a group here."

"I hope you don't mind. I was going to cut class short when Shelly said you were coming out, but the boys wanted to talk to you about bull riding, watch you work on the barrel, and just meet you. You're famous, you know."

Rusty blushed, but didn't respond. What do you say to that?

"What do you want to work on first or do you want to talk to the boys?" Logan put his hand on Rusty's shoulder. "I hope you don't mind talking to them. I would appreciate it and you would make some real loyal fans if you did."

"I don't mind." They walked closer to the group as he noticed a few boys whispering to each other, pointing at him, and then whispering again. He wished he could hear what they were saying. Were they impressed with riding? Were they sorry he'd been hurt, but wondering if he would ever be able to ride again? "Hi there." A chorus of hellos greeted him. "I hear a few of you might have some questions?"

One young man sitting on the fence raised his hand. "Are you going to be able to go back on the circuit come January?"

There is was, the ultimate question, the one even he didn't really know the answer to, but he was going to give it one hell of a shot. "At this point, I don't know. That's my plan, but my leg is still in bad shape. The break wasn't as clean as I first was lead to believe so it's taking a long time to heal. I'm here today to get some time on the barrel to see if I can grip it with my legs without too much discomfort before I try to get on a real bull."

Another raised his hand. "You were on the way to winning the championship this year, Rusty. How did it feel to watch Levi Bond take that away from you?"

"He really didn't take it away from me. He earned that title. He did some awesome riding over the course of several months to gain that title, even with a bum shoulder. Levi is a friend and as a friend, I wished him the best. I went to the finals myself to watch and hang out with the guys. It was a great time, and I wouldn't wish ill on anyone on the circuit. Most of us are good friends, and even though we are competitors in the arena, we never want to see each other hurt."

An older boy standing on the ground by the barrel, stepped forward. Rusty could tell he had a chip on his shoulder from a mile away. The kid looked cocky and self-absorbed, bad combination for anyone looking to go head-to-head with a mad bull. "How do you feel about Levi being gay and hooking up with Curt Walsh? I hear they are lovers."

The other boys giggled while others looked down at the dirt beneath their feet.

"What Levi and Curt have between them is their business. I don't comment on others' lives, just like what I do in my personal life is my business. I will say one thing, if they are happy, then so be it."

"But they are queers."

"Queer is a term given by people who don't understand how two people of the same sex can love each other. I suggest you do your homework, get to know someone who is gay, and find out how they feel about that term. You'd be surprised. Gays are just like you and me, and who knows which of you in this group might be gay." He stepped toward the barrel. "Let's ride."

* * * *

Lucas sat nursing a beer as he listened to reruns of the world finals on television. CBS was playing them over and over this week, but he didn't care. He knew every ride, every win, and every buck-off by heart. He'd been there and watched each one. Nope, right now, he needed to figure out what the hell he was going to do about the fact that Nick was working with Rusty, one his past lover, and the other his current fuck buddy.

His relationship with Nick had been a tumultuous one. They'd met at The Rusty Nail one Saturday night after he'd come home from a particularly bad riding weekend. He'd been bucked off his first ride and then again on his second ride, cutting his weekend short. Coming home meant dealing with his family as well. He had a sister and brother as well as his parents. He knew his parents wouldn't understand his attraction to another man just like the town of Albuquerque wouldn't understand. His family would disown them if they knew.

He'd never revealed his relationship with Nick to anyone. They'd kept it a secret for a long time, but when he'd said those three nasty words, Nick had bailed. He'd said he didn't want a long term relationship. They were okay as lovers, but nothing more. He wasn't in love with Lucas.

It had hurt, a lot. He'd spent days in the bottom of a bottle, even missing several riding events over those torturous weeks after Nick had walked, but he'd survived and even realized what he'd thought was love, wasn't. You can't really fall in love with someone who doesn't return your feelings.

The situation now was his attraction to Rusty. What was he going to do about it and how would they keep any kind of sexual relationship a secret on the circuit? People were kind of funny about guys being gay in such a close knit, all male community like bull riding.

If what they said was true about Levi and Curt Walsh, maybe he'd talk to them and see how they were going to handle it.

He downed the rest of his beer in a few gulps, before climbing to his feet to get another one. He wasn't sure what he was going to do. In his heart, he knew he had a major attraction to Rusty and it wasn't even on the same level as his attraction for Nick had been. Rusty had everything he wanted in a lover, and they'd only been together once. What would it be like to be together all the time? If they became traveling partners on the road during the season, they could fuck every night, and no one on the circuit would be the wiser. Guys shared rooms frequently. It wouldn't be anything new. They could keep their sexuality and situation a secret from the other riders. That was important to him, anonymity would have to be maintained.

Lucas got another beer from the refrigerator and resumed his place on the sofa. He really needed to do some work on a syllabus for a class he had on Monday at the local community college. History 101. This was a new gig for him since he usually taught high school level. The dean of the school called him last week and said his history teacher would be out for a week with her husband and he needed a sub. Lucas didn't have anything lined up, so he'd said yes. His next assignment at the high school wasn't until the following week. It would be interesting to see the difference between college level students and high school students. He didn't know which he'd like better. High school kids were a different breed and it took handling them with kid gloves most of the time to get them to do what they needed to do, especially for a substitute, but college level students were paying to be there. They had a different motivational factor.

The screen zeroed in on the chute where the last rider was getting ready. He watched as the rider wrapped his hand, gave the nod, and the world exploded in a frenzy of hooves, spinning, and lurching. He sat forward on the seat. This was it. Levi rode for the championship. It was all or nothing on this ride. The standings were too close to call, but if Levi didn't hang on for eight seconds, he would drop into second place and another would win the title.

Lucifer's Chaos. Even the name of the bull struck fear in the riders of the circuit. Every rider had been given a chance on the bull, most had not succeeded in riding him. Would Levi?

Lucas watched as the bull twirled, whirled, kicked, and did everything he could to unseat Levi. As the buzzer sounded, Levi unhooked his hand from the bull rope, jumped clear, and pumped his fists in the air. He'd done it! He'd ridden for the full eight.

Even though Lucas knew the outcome of the ride, the score, and the fact that Levi's took home the title, the buckle, and the check, excitement skittered down his back. This is what he lived for, the adrenaline surge that came from riding. Some riders could feel it just watching and he was one of those lucky bastards able to get the blood pumping through his body, even if he was only sitting in front of a TV or in the stands. It helped that he knew most of the riders personally.

Lucas sat back against the couch and watched the last few minutes where they gave Levi the check before he grabbed the remote and flipped off the television. He was itching to ride. He hated these months where the break kept them from competing. The high that came from riding was as addicting as any drug on the market.

His thoughts drifted back to Rusty. What was he doing this afternoon? Working the ranch, doing the books, or sitting around the house wishing he was riding like Lucas was.

He grabbed his cell phone out of his pants pocket and flipped through the contacts. When he got to Rusty's number, his finger hovered over the button to call him. After the way he left this morning, he probably shouldn't. *Give it a couple of days.*

He set the phone down on the coffee table and wiped his hands on the thighs of his jeans, not that they were sweaty or anything thinking about Rusty, but he had itchy palms. He needed to do something physical. Maybe he would go up to his workout room and lift weights. Yeah, that sounded like a good idea before he got to work on the syllabus for the class he needed to do. He usually didn't have to do the syllabus since the other teacher would be back in a week, but she'd asked him to get the class prepared since she wasn't sure how long she would really be out. He might end up teaching for the whole two months of his break. It would be different, he guessed, but interesting teaching at the college level.

First things first, work off this energy.

He climbed to his feet and headed to his room to change into some gym shorts, a t-shirt, and some tennis shoes.

When he opened the door to his workout room, he smiled. He had top of the line gym equipment. Free weights, an elliptical, weight bench, and all the accoutrements anyone could ask for to work out with.

After doing hundreds of reps of different exercises, he got on the elliptical, working his legs and cardiovascular for over an hour. Sweat poured from his temples and down his chest. His breath came out in hard pants as he continued to pumps his legs. It was good for them to be in shape when they needed to grip the sides of the bull as they held on.

He needed this.

By the time he finished, he was physically wiped out, but pumped up at the same time.

A shower would feel good on his sweaty, hot muscles.

He pulled the t-shirt over his head, wiping the sweat from his chest, neck and face with it as he headed toward his bedroom for some clean clothes. A cool shower would feel like heaven.

Stripping off the rest of his clothes, he walked naked into the bathroom to turn on the shower. A cool spray of water came from the head with a twist of his wrist.

He loved his bathroom with the travertine tile, big mirrors, open walk-in shower, and rain showerhead. He'd designed it himself when he'd had the house built. He stepped back and took in his reflection in the mirror. The blond hair on his head lay plastered to his skull with sweat, his blue eyes stared back from the mirror as his gaze traveled down over his pecs, flat abdomen, long, thick cock, and trim legs. He didn't think he was a bad specimen of a human being, so why was it so hard to find someone to spend the rest of his life with? *Wait a minute. Who said I wanted someone permanent? I don't need that kind of headache.*

He shook his head as he turned to face the shower and step under the spray. The cold water made goose bumps appear on his arms, but it felt good to his heated skin. He grabbed the shampoo from the shelf and began scrubbing his sweaty scalp until bubbles ran down his chest and abdomen. With a sigh, he moved back under the water, letting it cascade over his head, washing away the bubbles until the water ran clear. Next came the body wash. It was one of his favorite scents and one he used even in his aftershave.

A smile crossed his lips when he remembered Rusty stopping to sniff him.

Rusty.

What he wouldn't give to have him here with him right now, sharing the shower, fucking him against the wall, sucking off his cock on his knees with the water pounding down on them from behind.

Hmm. The thought was intriguing.

Lucas closed his eyes as he palmed his cock slick with body wash, and stroked it up and down. He could totally imagine Rusty on his knees in front of him, sucking his cock between his lips. A moan escaped Lucas's lips as the imaginary Rusty got him hard as a rock.

Before he had a chance to enjoy the blow job, Rusty pushed him against the wall of the shower, pulled his hips out so he could reach his ass, and penetrated him using the soap as a lubricant.

As Rusty fucked him from behind, his own cock got painfully hard. He needed to come badly.

"Not yet," Rusty whispered in his ear.

"I need to."

"Wait. It'll be better if you wait."

"Fuck, Rusty, you're killing me here."

"What a way to die, my friend."

Rusty continued to pound into him, bringing him up on his toes as his cock stretched him to the fullest he'd ever felt. Lucas stroked his cock as Rusty's breath came out faster and faster. His rhythm became disjointed. Lucas knew he was close.

"Come now, Lucas. Paint the wall with your cum."

Lucas exploded in a rush of semen, squirting the side of the shower with white as his orgasm overtook him.

When he opened his eyes, his cock was getting soft, and he needed to wash the cum from his abdomen and hand. *Wow. That was pretty intense. Now if I only had the real thing.* He exhaled through pursed lips as he stepped back under the shower spray.

Once everything was clean, he shut the water off, grabbed a towel from the rack and dried himself off. With the towel wrapped around his hips, he headed back into his bedroom to get dressed.

His doorbell rang just as he was making his way to his bed. Shrugging his shoulders, he headed downstairs to see who was at the door.

He peeked through the curtain and smiled. Rusty stood on his stoop.

After he adjusted the towel on his hips, he opened the door, leaning against the frame as casually as he could. He felt anything but casual having the man he'd just fantasized about in the shower, standing on his porch. "What's up?"

"I wanted to share what I did this afternoon with you." He opened the screen, glancing down at the towel riding low on Lucas's hips. "Did I catch you at a bad time?"

"Nope. Just got out of the shower. Come on in." He walked into the kitchen and grabbed a beer from the refrigerator for both he and Rusty. "Beer?"

"Sure."

"Let me put some clothes on. I'll be right back."

"Don't get dressed on my account."

Lucas glanced at Rusty, a grin spreading across his lips. "I'm sure we could find something to do, but let's talk first."

"Okay." Rusty took a seat on the couch, popped open his beer, and took a sip.

Lucas wanted nothing more than to drag Rusty off into the bedroom with him, let him fuck the hell out of him, and then they could talk, but after this morning's incident, he figured he'd better calm down and get some things out in the open before they did that.

"I'll be right back."

He came back a few minutes later, jeans, t-shirt, and bare feet. He didn't want to be too dressed in case they got down to fucking soon. He knew he wanted to, anyway. "So what's up?" he asked, taking a seat on the opposite end of the couch.

"Did you know there is a bull riding school here in Albuquerque?"

"No." He took a sip of his beer. "Where?"

"It's called the Double L and it's out past my place on 314. Nice people. Logan Tyler owns it. He let me get on their practice bull for a bit after I spent some time on the barrel."

"How do you feel?"

"Sore, but good. I think I'll be back in January, no problem."

"Don't rush it, Rusty. Take the time you need."

"What? You don't want me back?"

"I would love to see you on the back of a bull again, my friend, but don't hurt yourself trying to do it before you're ready, that's all. You could do some permanent damage if you try to come back too soon."

Rusty's eyes were wide with excitement. "Sorry. I'm just excited."

Lucas smiled. "I can tell. I don't think I've seen you this hyped up in a long time. It's like you've got your mojo back."

"I do. I'm ready to ride. I think I'll call Mr. Campbell and see about getting on some of his bulls."

Lucas sat forward, focusing his gaze on Rusty. "Mr. Campbell?"

"Yeah. Mr. Campbell of Rocking C Bucking Bulls."

"I don't understand."

"I sat next to him on the plane coming home from Vegas. He gave me his card. He said I could practice on some of his bulls after we got home."

"Seriously?"

"Yeah. I'm going to call him and see what we can arrange."

"Whoa. Now hold on, Rusty. Being on some up and coming bulls is totally different than getting on one that is circuit qualified. You probably need to slow down a bit."

"Why do I get the feeling you are trying to dissuade me?"

"I am. I'm trying to protect you."

"I don't need protecting, Lucas, I need your support."

"Rusty. You and I are friends. I'm not going to bullshit you into thinking you are one hundred percent ready to go back. You know you aren't. You're still limping and still taking pain pills regularly, right?"

"Yeah."

"Then you aren't ready. Take it slow. Practice. Get on some bulls. Don't rush things though."

Rusty dropped his gaze to the floor as he rubbed his sore thigh. "I know. I know, you're right, but I felt so good today."

"That's fantastic, but you'll probably be even more sore tomorrow than you have been."

The sigh leaving Rusty's lips made Lucas feel like shit. He didn't want to burst his friend's bubble, but he didn't want to see him get hurt either. If it meant giving him a reality check, so be it.

Chapter Seven

Lucas leaned on the metal railing with one foot propped on the bottom rung as he watched Rusty get ready to ride. For now, it was only a barrel, but he couldn't help but hold his breath when the bucking started. One of Nick's hands worked the back of the barrel up and down simulating the bucking action of a real live bull.

It wasn't anything close to the real thing. This thought came from experience. A real bull twisted, twirled, bucked, kicked, and then reversed back the other way so fast your head would snap with each movement. Your arm could be ripped out of the socket with one vicious twist of the bull's body.

Rusty looked good though. His body flowed well with the rocking of the barrel, his arm whipped back and forth in perfect rhythm. His thighs gripped the side of the barrel strongly, the muscles bulging with each movement. Maybe it was time for him to get on some real rank bulls.

Lucas shook his head as he let his gaze focus on the dirt beneath their feet. He was afraid, terrified really. When Rusty had taken that spill, he thought he would throw up as he watched them wheel his friend out of the arena on a stretcher. He knew the break could be a career ending situation, but he'd been more concerned about Rusty's state of mind. Rusty wasn't ready to retire from what he knew. His gaze returned to his friend on the bull.

"Harder. Push me. I need it."

The concentration on Rusty's face told Lucas he was in pain with every movement of the barrel. "Don't you think you need a bit of a break?"

Rusty didn't lift his head as he answered, "Hell no. I need to keep going."

"You've been at it for over an hour."

When Rusty finally locked his gaze with Lucas's, he could see the determination reflected in Rusty's eyes. He would be ready for January, come hell or high water. He wasn't giving up and he wasn't going to stop until he was on top again.

A groan escaped Rusty's lips as he lost his balance on the barrel and slipped off, falling into the dirt with a sickening thud. "Fuck!"

"You okay?"

"Yeah." Rusty climbed to his feet before he pounded on his chaps to dislodge the dirt from the fall. He rotated his head to loosen the muscles in his neck. "My legs aren't strong enough."

"Yes, they are, Rusty. You were holding on great."

"Not good enough. My legs feel like Jello right now."

"Don't you have a weight room at the house?"

"Yeah. I guess I'll be doing some leg presses when we get back inside."

Nick glanced his way before focusing back on Rusty. "You'll be ready in January, Rusty. It just takes some time. You had a bad break and it's barely healed. You might be pushing too hard."

"I only have a few weeks to get back into shape. I can't pussy out. I have to prove I'm ready when we start again. Practicing is the only way. Now get ready. I'm going again."

"All right then. I'll do what I can to help you."

"Me too. You know I'll do whatever you need me to do, Rusty," Lucas added to the conversation. He wanted Rusty to know he had his back no matter whether he felt uncomfortable with Nick around or not.

Rusty climbed back onto the barrel, wrapped his hand in the bull rope, and nodded for Nick to begin the rocking motion. Lucas watched his every move so he could critique it for Rusty when they went back in the house. His insight into the movement of his hand, the position of his body, and the way he kept himself centered would be invaluable. It was the least he could do for the guy who had taken up residence in his thoughts on a daily basis.

Soon, he would have to figure out what they were, boyfriends, friends, lovers, or fuck buddies. Whatever it was, he wanted Rusty more than ever.

He had to physically pull his thoughts back to the situation at hand or he would find himself reliving their rousing bout of sex and wishing he was right there again. *Maybe this afternoon I can get some pounding sex going on.*

His gaze wandered to Nick. The whole situation with his former lover being here had his nerves on edge. He didn't love Nick anymore, of that he was certain, but he still felt uncomfortable being around him on a regular basis.

"How'd that look, Lucas?" Rusty asked as the barrel came to a halt.

"Great."

"I need more than that, buddy. Give me a critique with some details."

"Okay. Your balance is off center a little to the left. Your hand in the rope looked good. Your balance hand wasn't moving enough. You're a bit stiff in your seat."

Rusty's eyes narrowed as he looked at Lucas. "Is that all?"

"You asked."

"I know. Sorry. I can't seem to loosen up."

"What's got you so tense?"

A little smile played on Rusty's lips. "I bet you can figure it out."

Lucas did a double take at Rusty's blatant flirting. Was he really interpreting that smile the right way? Was Rusty coming onto him right there in front of Nick?

"I'll help you work those kinks out a little later. For now, you'll have to figure out how to loosen your abdominal muscles, your back, and your chest on your own."

"Well damn."

"When are you supposed to go over to Campbell's place?"

"Next week. He's going to let me on some of his bulls." Rusty centered himself before looking back over his shoulder. "I have a meeting with one of his friends about sponsorship too."

"That would be great."

"Yeah, I could use a little more financial help with expenses and such. These trips all over the country with rooms, meals, and shit, get expensive."

"You were bringing in the big money last year though."

"I know, but I lost out on the last few months of the season. Those checks only go so far when you have a place to maintain, animals to feed, and all that stuff."

"I know what you mean. My house isn't paid for yet either."

Rusty nodded toward Nick. "Let's go."

Lucas kept an eye on Rusty as he continued to ride the barrel. Maybe he was ready to get on some bulls. Lucas wasn't sure. He'd have to see him ride one before he could come to that conclusion, but the whole thing bothered Lucas too. He hoped Rusty wasn't pushing too hard too fast.

The afternoon wore on until the sun began to dip in the evening sky when Rusty finally called it a day. "I'm done for now. Thanks, Nick."

"You're welcome. Are you going to ride some more tomorrow? I'll be in town with the latest shipment of feed so I won't be able to work it for you, but Lucas probably can since he seems to be hanging around here a lot more."

"Listen, Nick. I know about you and Lucas, but it's in the past. Lucas and I are friends, so yeah, he's going to hang out here. If you have a problem with that, say so now."

Nick tipped his hat back on his head. "Nope. No problem."

"Good." Rusty grabbed his rope from the ground and walked toward where Lucas stood at the gate.

The slow roll of his hips made Lucas's mouth water. "I don't know about you, but I'm starving. Do you want to go into town and get a burger?"

Rusty unbuckled his chaps from around his legs so he could work them down his legs before tossing them over the railing. "Sounds good." Rusty turned back for a moment. "Nick, I'll see you in the morning."

"Sure, boss."

Rusty started toward the house with Lucas on his heels. The evening sky had turned to a burnt orange as the sun began its final descent behind the hills. Several lights were on inside the house, illuminating the front windows with the white curtains shifting in the breeze. Lucas really liked Rusty's house. It was homey and welcoming. His own seemed stark and plain in comparison. Rusty had really made his place a sanctuary to return to after the long weeks on the road.

"I really like your place, Rusty."

"Thanks."

When they walked through the big wooden door, Lucas was caught unaware as Rusty turned around, grabbed him by the front of his t-shirt and slammed his mouth down on his lips. *Holy fuck!* His dick jerked to life in an instant, hardening to painful within seconds. Rusty shoved his tongue between Lucas's lips, stroking his own in a primal dance of desire. Lucas fisted Rusty's hard on in his hand, yanking back until their mouths separated.

Rusty was panting so hard, the puffs of air warmed Lucas's lips. "What?"

"Where the hell did that come from?"

Rusty stepped back. "I've watched you leaning on that fence all day, your jeans tight across your cock, your arms bulging in the sleeves of your t-shirt, your chest pulling the material taut across your pecs, and I've been hard as a damned rock. Do you have any idea how difficult it is to ride when your dick is straining against the front of your jeans?"

"Yep. Been there before."

"Then I suggest you strip off those clothes and we get to fucking."

"No beating around the bush with you, huh?"

"Not tonight."

"I thought you were hungry?" Lucas asked, his gaze trailing down Rusty's face until it locked on his lips. The taste wasn't enough. He needed more.

"I am, but I figure we can fuck now, go get a burger, and then fuck again afterwards."

Fucking sounded good to him.

Lucas yanked on the button at Rusty's waist, freeing the waistband enough he could grab the tab for the zipper and slowly pull it down. He wanted to tease Rusty a bit since everything seemed to happen so fast before. It would be nice to have this man beneath him begging for release. Lucas smiled at the raw desire reflected in Rusty's eyes. His cheeks were flushed, his chest rose and fell with each straining breath, and his hands were fisted in Lucas's shirt as he tried to get closer.

When Lucas pulled Rusty's jeans and boxers down, letting them pool at his feet, a sigh escaped Rusty's lips. Rock hard flesh bobbed against Rusty's abdomen. Pre-cum glistened on the slit. "Horny, are we?"

"You have no idea."

Rusty toed off his boots before pushing the pooled material of his jeans off his feet.

"What do you want, Rusty?"

"I want you to suck me."

Lucas palmed Rusty's cock in his hand, sliding it up and down in a slow torturous rhythm. "Like this?" He knew what

Rusty wanted, but he needed to hear the man say it with all that raging need in his voice.

"No. I want your mouth."

"Are you sure you can handle my mouth?"

"God, please. I'm dying here."

Lucas leaned in, trailing his mouth along Rusty's neck, biting and nipping as he moved down. The buttons on the front of Rusty's shirt, popped off as Lucas yanked on the material, exposing his chest. Lucas continued down the firm pecs beneath his mouth until Rusty moaned softly. He had him right where he wanted him.

As Lucas dropped to his knees, he grasped Rusty's cock in his hand, fisting the glorious hardness before he buried his nose in the crease between Rusty's balls and his thigh. The musky scent of desire reached his nose. A quick swipe of his tongue around Rusty's balls had his lover moaning loudly.

Rusty fisted his hands in Lucas's hair, guiding him toward the crown of his cock.

When the purple head disappeared between Lucas's lips, Rusty shuddered. As he took the entire length in his mouth, Rusty's knees almost gave out. Lucas backed off, letting Rusty's cock pop from his mouth. "On the couch."

Rusty walked with a wobbling gate over to the leather sofa and slid onto the cushion.

Lucas wasted no time following him down so he could take Rusty's cock into his mouth again.

Still fully clothed, Lucas made a meal of Rusty's cock in short order, tonguing the veins running around the hard flesh, and working the full length with his mouth as he palmed Rusty's balls.

"I'm gonna come."

"No you aren't. Not until I have your cock in my ass." Lucas got to his feet, toed off his boots, pushed his jeans to the floor, and then whipped his shirt over his head. His cock ached with need, but all he could think about was Rusty buried deep. "We need lube."

"In the bedroom."

"Do you want to go in there to finish this?"

"Yeah, let's do that."

They grabbed their clothes from the floor before they both walked into Rusty's bedroom naked as the day they were born. The brown rustic décor was a sight for sore eyes for Lucas. He loved having the different hues to compare and contrast. For now, he wouldn't have time to admire the bed other than to be on it with Rusty.

"I'm so fucking hard, I hurt," Rusty said, dropping his pile of clothes to the floor while moving toward the nightstand. "Let me grab the lube and a condom."

Following suit, Lucas threw his stuff toward the corner and nervously sat on the bed as he waited for Rusty. Now that they were here and going to fuck, he wasn't as brave as he made it sound. He wanted Rusty so badly his balls ached. It had been some time since they'd been together and he hadn't been with anyone else in the meantime. He watched Rusty roll the condom over his cock and slick it up with the lube in his hand. His mouth went dry as the ritual continued until Rusty had it shiny and slippery. Lucas licked his lips trying desperately to get a little liquid into his mouth.

"Roll over with your belly on the bed and your feet on the floor."

Lucas did as he was told, positioning himself with his legs apart, his ass up, and his toes barely touching the floor.

The next thing he felt was Rusty's cock bumping at his back hole. He held his breath as Rusty slowly fed his cock into Lucas's ass, past the ring of muscles at the opening, only to be buried deep within a matter of seconds. He exhaled on a sharp sigh.

"Okay?"

"Yeah. My God, you feel amazing."

"Fuck yeah."

"Go slow."

"I'm not hurting you, am I?"

"No, but it's been a while. I want to enjoy this."

Rusty pulled his cock out until it was barely inside before pushing back in. The slow rocking motion of his hips drove his cock in and out in the most torturous fucking of Lucas's life. The amazing thing was, the feel of Rusty's cock buried deep touch something in Lucas's soul, like he'd found the missing puzzle piece he'd been looking for all his life.

As Rusty began to increase the speed of his thrusts, Lucas's balls drew up against his groin in preparation for his own orgasm. He gritted his teeth against the sensation. Holding on for longer would make it that much better, he knew, but it might kill him in the process.

Rusty leaned over Lucas's back. "I know you are holding back. I can feel you clenching around my cock. The feeling is amazing, but right now, I'm going to fuck you so hard, all that fantastic cream will explode out the end of your dick like you haven't come so hard in your life."

The rapid thrust of Rusty's hips shoved his cock into Lucas's ass until they were banging the bed against the wall in a steady *thump, thump, thump* rhythm.

Fuck, I'm gonna die! "Rusty, please."

"Please what, Lucas? Fuck me harder?" A dry, humorous laugh escaped Rusty's mouth. "Okay, I can do that."

Rusty slammed his rutting pelvis against Lucas's ass until Lucas thought his head would explode. His cock ached with the need to come. His balls would probably shrivel up and die if he didn't orgasm soon, but something was holding him back, something he couldn't quite place. Then it happened, the one thing that would make the whole experience complete, a sharp nip of teeth at the slope where his neck and his shoulder met.

The bite was hard enough to mark him in a possessive way that should he decide to find someone else in the near future, they would know that he belonged to Rusty. The pain sent him careening over the threshold of control he'd held onto his orgasm with as cum shot out the end of his dick, painting white streaks across Rusty's blanket. He tossed his head back and yelled, "Fuck yeah!"

Lucas felt Rusty shudder as his own orgasm overcame him, and he slumped over Lucas's back.

"Holy shit."

"You can say that again."

Rusty slowly removed his softened cock, slipped off the condom and tied the end before he sat down on the bed next to Lucas. "That was amazing."

"Yes it was."

A sharp, stinging slap on Lucas's ass brought him upright, flipping over until his stinging butt cheek rested on the comforter. "What the hell did you do that for?"

"You seem to get off on a little pain. I thought I'd see what else you might be into." The grin on Rusty's face softened the blow—a little.

"That fucking hurt."

"That's the idea. Pain brings pleasure in some circles."

"What the hell have you been watching on your computer? Gay porn?"

"Of course, but even better. A little bondage and submission. You should see some of the shit that's online."

"I can imagine."

Rusty shook his head. "No, trust me, you can't. There is some really weird shit on there."

"Don't be planning to use that crap on me, buddy."

Rusty stood and dropped the used condom into the trashcan at the side of the bed before he turned back toward Lucas. He softly touched Lucas's shoulder where he'd bitten him. "You liked it when I bit your shoulder."

"Yes I did, but that doesn't mean I want you to whip me or some other weird stuff you saw online."

"You don't want to experiment?"

Lucas had to think about that one for a moment. He had enjoyed the bite at the exact time he'd lost his control on his own pleasure and shot his load, but he wasn't too sure about getting into whips, handcuffs, and different things like that. Maybe if Rusty would let him try some things on him? That might be cool. He could think of a few situations that might be kind of fun. "Can I do it to you?"

"Maybe. We'll see what happens. I do want to try a few things that I saw. They seem interesting. Nothing too strange though." Rusty slipped on some clean boxers and jeans. "I'm starving. Are you ready for that burger?"

Lucas grabbed his jeans, shirt, and underwear from the floor. "You bet."

A wicked grin graced Rusty's lips as he slowly walked toward him. When he leaned in and brought their lips together in a soul-stealing kiss, Lucas could do nothing more than hang on for the ride. What a ride it was turning out to be.

Chapter Eight

Morning broke over the horizon with sunshine blazing across the fields. Rusty stood outside on his porch with a cup of coffee in hand, watching the beautiful view. This is what life was made of, his land, his cattle, and his soul bound to this piece of property. If he only had the one person he was coming to care about more than anything by his side.

Sex between them had been off the charts since they'd come together a few weeks before. Lucas had been spending more and more time at Rusty's place after his work days at the college had finished. They'd become almost domesticated, but not quite. Lucas ate at his house, slept in his bed, worked the fields with him when he wasn't teaching, and had become such an integral part of Rusty's life, he couldn't quite imagine him not in it.

Rusty took another sip of his coffee before sitting the cup on the porch rail. He'd left Lucas sleeping soundly in his bed after a rousing bout of morning sex.

Today was Saturday. Lucas didn't have to leave at all today.

His gut tightened. Today, they were supposed to have dinner with his family. Dread filled his soul. Could they continue to keep their relationship a secret around his parents and siblings? He wasn't sure if he wanted to keep up with the charade of friendship or let his family in on what their relationship actually was.

Of course, he wasn't even sure what it was anymore. Were they friends only? They were lovers, yes, but neither of them had admitted to the other any deeper feelings even though Rusty knew his feelings were becoming more than friendship alone.

He knew his father would never understand and neither would Russell. His younger siblings might and his mother probably would. She always seemed so forgiving and accepting of anything he did over the years. It was his father who would take the belt to them should they mess up and do something very wrong.

Once, he'd stolen a game from a video store when he was smaller. His father had found it when he'd come into his room to get him ready for bed. When he'd emptied his pockets, the game fell out.

The disappointment in his father's gaze had been his undoing. The belt hurt, yes, but he'd learned a lesson that night about a father's love. His was conditional upon being the good kid. Rusty had turned into the epitome of the perfect child until he'd turned eighteen and left home to become a bull rider.

His father had never understood his need for the dirt, the adrenaline of the ride, and the roar of the crowd.

It was time to come clean with his family. He was tired of pretending. He was tired of hiding his sexuality. He was tired of being something he wasn't. They would have to deal with it.

A set of hands went around his middle and pulled him back against a solid chest.

"What are you thinking about?"

"The dinner with my family today."

"And?"

"I plan to tell them about us."

The hands disappeared.

"What about us?" Lucas asked, taking a seat on the white swing at the end of the porch.

Rusty turned so he could face his lover and take in his reaction to the news of what he wanted to reveal. "I know you aren't comfortable with people knowing you are gay. That's your choice, Lucas, but my choice is to let my family in on my sexual preferences. If you don't want me to tell them about our relationship, whatever it is, then I won't, but I need to get this off my chest. I don't want to hide it anymore from anyone, much less my family."

"How do you think they'll react?"

"I'm not sure. I think my father and Russell will disown me, but that's okay. I'm not the perfect child I tried to be growing up. I've come to realize I'm me and if they can't accept me the way I am, then it's their problem, not mine. I think my mom will be fine with it and so will the younger brothers. I think they will support me in whatever I choose to do because they love me."

"You don't think your father or Russell love you?"

"Oh, they do in their own way, but for my father it will be a blow to his own manhood. How could he birth a child who likes being with someone of the same sex? The prodigal child. The oldest son. That sort of thing. Of course, if what Russell says is true, he's pretty much written me off anyway because I'm not around to run the family place. Russell will hate me because it will bring into question his own sexuality. How could we have shared the same womb with one of us being straight and one being gay? Russell already hates me anyway, so whatever, I guess."

A frown marred Lucas's face as he glanced down at the wooden porch between his bare feet. "I'm sorry, Rusty, but I think you are making a huge mistake. You know people in this town don't approve of the gay lifestyle, not at all. I'm afraid you're going to cause more grief than you will acceptance for yourself."

"You're entitled to your opinion, of course, but this is me. I can't help how others feel. I can only live my life how I want to." Rusty took a seat next to Lucas on the swing. "The question is how will this affect our relationship?"

"I'm not sure. I don't want people to know I'm gay."

"Come on, Lucas. You go to the only gay bar in town. You've had a relationship with Nick. I'm sure people figured it out when you were seen together."

"Not really. We kept it quiet."

"Well, I'm not going to keep silent anymore. People will have to take me as I am." He sat back against the side of the swing and turned to face Lucas a little more so he could see his lover's face. "I want to talk to Levi and Curt too. I want to be open on the circuit about who I am."

"Damn. You really are going all out there, aren't you? Telling your family as well as being openly gay on the bull rider's circuit."

"They seem to be okay with Levi and Curt being together. Why wouldn't they be okay with me?"

"I don't think they are as accepting as you think they are. Levi and Curt probably put up with a lot of talk and stuff that we aren't aware of."

"Maybe, but this is my life. This is who I am."

"What if they force you off the circuit?"

"They can't do that. It's discrimination."

"True, it is, but they can make it look like something else. What if all your sponsors pull their money when they find out?"

Rusty hadn't thought of that. What if they did? Would it kill his career? Maybe, but he had to take his chances on it and be who he needed to be. "I'll have to live with it if they do."

"Don't you have an appointment with Mr. Campbell's buddy today to talk sponsorships?"

"Yeah and we are supposed to go out to Mr. Campbell's place and ride some bulls tomorrow."

"I hope you know what you're doing, Rusty. I think you're making a huge mistake on this, but you have to do whatever you feel is the right thing."

"So, do you want me to tell my family we are in a relationship?"

"Are we?"

"Are we what?"

"In a relationship?"

"I kind of thought we were. You've been spending more time over here than you have at your own place. I mean, at least we are fuck buddies, right?"

"I guess you could say that, yeah."

Even though Rusty's feelings ran deeper everyday he was around Lucas, he wasn't about to let his lover know, not yet anyway. He wanted Lucas to admit they were more to each other than fuck buddies. "If you don't want me to say anything, that's fine. It's none of my family's business what goes on in my house."

"I wish you wouldn't bring me into this."

"That's fine. I'll abide by your wishes."

"Thanks."

"Are you going to go with me to talk to the sponsor?"

"I think you should go alone. After all, he is interested in you and your riding career. It has nothing to do with me."

Disappointment zipped through him. Obviously, Lucas didn't feel the same about him as he felt about Lucas. If it was Lucas's career hanging in the balance, he'd be all over it, supporting him and standing by him no matter what. "All right." Rusty glanced out across the front yard to see a truck hauling ass down his driveway. It was too early for visitors. He climbed to his feet to await the coming storm when he recognized his father's truck as it came to a skidding halt in front of his gate.

His dad had no more than slammed the truck's door when he yelled across the yard, "You're a fucking faggot!"

Oh shit. Rusty took the two steps from his porch to meet his father in the yard. "Dad. I can explain."

"Explain what, Rusty. I heard from someone in town you were seen at that God damn faggot watering hole. Deny it if you can."

"I can't. I was there, yes." He glanced at Lucas who had remained in the swing, his face white and his hands shaking.

"Why, Rusty? Why would you be seen there? Are you trying to hurt me? Our family?"

"Listen, Dad. This is something I wanted to bring up at dinner this evening, but since you are here and know about the bar, I might as well tell you. You aren't going to like it one bit and I know what you are going to say, but I can't help what I am. Yes, Dad, I'm gay."

His father's eyes widened as his face blanched white. His hands were grasped in tight fists by his side. "You're gay as in you have sex with other men?" he whispered.

"Yes."

His father glanced over his shoulder toward the porch where Lucas still sat on the swing.

Before Rusty could react, his father swung his fist, connecting with Rusty's jaw and knocking him to the ground. He climbed on top of Rusty, pounding at his face as Rusty tried to guard himself from the blows. "My son is no queer! If I have to, I will beat it out of you. Obviously, I didn't beat you enough as a child."

Rusty felt the weight being removed from his chest as Lucas drug his father off him.

"Stop it!" Lucas held his father by the arms as he struggled against Lucas's hold.

Unable to really see much out of his rapidly swelling eyes, he tried to stand and wobbled as he got his bearings. "I'm sorry, Dad. Being gay isn't wrong. Beating the shit out of me is not going to change who I am." He wiped at the blood on his lips. "I am what I am and it's something you'll have to live with."

"You're not my son!" His father pulled away from Lucas's grasp. "Don't come to the house. Ever. I'm done with you. We are not your family anymore." His father spit in his face before turning on his heels and stomping off to where his truck sat. Gravel sprayed as he sped back down the driveway.

"Are you okay?" Lucas asked as he touched the large bruise Rusty knew was forming on his cheek.

"Yeah." He laughed ruefully as he wiped the spittle of his face. "That went well, eh?"

"About what you expected?"

"Yes, but I was hoping I would be on his turf and not mine. I wanted to be able to see my mother, talk to her, talk to the boys, and explain. I'll have to call her and have her meet me somewhere other than their house."

"Are you sure you want to continue to come out loud and proud about being gay? This should have told you something, Rusty. If your family isn't accepting, what makes you think those on the circuit will?'

"I don't, Lucas, but I can't help who I am."

Rusty headed for the house to wash his face. Disappointment in his father's reaction grated on his nerves. *I knew he would react that way. Why I'm so devastated by it, I don't know.* When he reached the hall, he turned left into his bedroom to grab a clean shirt since the one he had on now had blood on it.

He could barely see out of his eyes at the moment, but he hoped some ice packs would take most of the swelling down before he had to head over to meet the possible new sponsor. Explaining the bruises would be interesting. He could always say he took a bad blow from a bull, but he didn't think that would fly. Unless he'd taken a hit directly to the face by a bull's head, he probably wouldn't be able to explain them away.

The light in the bathroom flipped on with a small bit of pressure from his hand. He was almost afraid to look in the mirror.

He exhaled before moving toward the large glass on the wall.

Holy fuck!

Both eyes were bruised and swollen. His lip was cut and bleeding slightly. His right cheek had a huge bruise coming up nice and purple, and when he turned his head to the left, he noticed a large red slash across his neck.

His dad did one hell of a job rearranging his face for him.

Stubborn fool.

Not knowing whether he meant his father or himself, he wet a washcloth that had been lying on the sink, and then dabbed at the cut on his lip. He should probably count himself lucky that he didn't lose any teeth in the brawl.

After he'd cleaned himself up and put on a new shirt, he headed back down the hall to find Lucas sitting at his dining room table with a shot glass in his hand.

"A little early to drink, isn't it?"

"Not when you just watched someone you care about get the shit beat out of him by his own father, all because he admitted to being different than everyone else with a penis and a set of balls." Lucas downed the shot glass of whatever he'd poured in one swallow before he wiped the remaining liquid from his lips. He coughed a few times as he sucked air in through his lips to counteract the burning Rusty knew the liquid probably caused going down.

"Whiskey?"

"Yeah." Lucas lifted his gaze to meet Rusty's. "You look like shit."

"Thanks, buddy."

"You need to put some ice on those eyes."

Rusty walked toward the refrigerator and pulled open the top where the freezer held the typical stuff like ice cream, frozen vegetables, meat, and ice. The drawer next to the refrigerator held gallon size plastic bags, so he reached for one to put some ice in. After he zipped it closed, he went toward the living room to lie down on the couch. Once he settled himself across the cushions on the sofa, he laid the ice across his eyes with a sigh.

The scraping of the chair on the floor alerted him to Lucas's movement.

"You should have swung back."

"I can't hit my father."

"He was beating the shit out of you, Rusty. You could have defended yourself. No one would have held that against you."

"I guess."

"You know the news will be all over town before nightfall."

"Probably."

"It doesn't matter to you?"

"Not really. I'm surprised no one said anything before now. It's been over a week since we were in The Rusty Nail, Lucas, and it's a known gay bar."

"True."

"It doesn't matter. It would come out eventually and I feel better now that my dad knows." The phone on the table next to Rusty's head rang. "Can you get that?"

"Hello?" There was a pause in Lucas's voice. "Yes, ma'am. He's here. He's on the couch with some ice on his eyes." Another pause. "All right. Here he is."

Rusty felt the phone receiver next to his cheek, so he grabbed for it and held it to his ear. "Hello?"

"Rusty? Honey, are you okay?"

"Hi, Mom. Yes, I'm fine. Just bruised up a bit. How's Dad?"

"Listen to you, worried about your asshole father."

"Mom!"

"Well, he is. There is no reason for him to do what he did to you, Rusty, and for the record, it doesn't matter to me if you love someone of the opposite sex or the same sex. You are still my son and you always will be."

"Thanks, Mom. Did he tell my brothers?"

"Of course, he did. Russell stomped out of here headed for the barn. The last I saw him, he was riding hell-bent for leather toward the east pasture. John is upset. He hasn't said much, but

Junior and Thomas are supportive of you. They don't care who you love."

"I appreciate the support."

"Is Lucas your lover?"

"Yeah, but he doesn't want people to know about him so keep that tidbit to yourself, please."

"Sure, honey, even though it's pretty obvious when you two are together. It's hard to keep those kinds of feelings under wraps. I can see the love between you when you two are around each other."

"Uh…"

"What?"

"I wouldn't say it was that, Mom."

"Honey, it's very apparent when you look at him."

"Well, it's not something that has been discussed. Put it that way."

"Oh."

"I should go, Mom. I need to get ready to head over to talk to the sponsor Mr. Campbell wants me to meet."

"All right, son. Lots of luck and I hope things work out for the best between you and Lucas. I think you two are cute together."

"Thanks. I appreciate the support."

"I love you, Rusty. You do what is best for you and don't worry about your father. He'll come around."

"Bye, Mom."

"Bye, honey."

Rusty handed the receiver back to Luas and heard him hang it back up on the hook.

"Your mom is one hell of a lady."

"Don't I know it." Rusty sat up and swung his legs over the side of the couch. The ice bag dropped into his lap. "What time is it?"

"Only about seven. Why?"

"I need to get something to eat and more coffee. There are some chores that need to be done too, before I head over to Mr. Campbell's. The appointment with the sponsor is at ten."

"I'll help you get the animals fed, watered, and turned out. You probably can't see too well with those eyes almost swollen shut. You should rest on the couch with that ice on your face. I can do the chores in the barn."

"Would you?"

"Of course. It's the least I can do, Rusty. You've had my back on several occasions. I can help you. Besides, I've been helping for the last few weeks. I think I can handle this for one morning."

"All right. Just be sure to let Missy out of her stall into the big arena with her foal. She needs to run a bit and it will help the foal get his feet under him."

"He's a beautiful one too."

"Yes he is."

"Did you figure out a name for him?"

"Not yet but I'll bet he'll make some beautiful babies when the time comes."

"Yes he will."

Lucas shoved Rusty back down on the couch, put the ice over his eyes, and then moved away. Rusty could hear the banging of the screen door as he went outside and it made him smile. It was great to have Lucas here with him. He enjoyed the company out of bed and in, but the in was the best. They really were on the same wavelength when it came to making love and that's what it was to Rusty now.

He sighed as visions of their raucous bout of sex the night before played over in his mind.

He'd been washing his hair when he heard the swoosh of the door on the shower open. Not sure what to expect, he held his breath as he slowly continued to scrub his hair.

The warm slide of a tongue around his balls brought his cock to standing at attention in no time flat.

When warmth surrounded the head of his cock a second later, his breath had caught in his throat before exiting his mouth as a sigh. God, the feel of Lucas's mouth on him had driven him to full-blown aching hard on within seconds.

His asshole puckered tight at the thought of Lucas's cock plunging deep.

He wanted that more than anything in the world, at that very moment, and he couldn't wait to get it.

"Oh God."

Lucas ran his tongue around and around the head of Rusty's cock before he deep throated the entire length to the point where it bumped at the back of his throat. When he swallowed, Rusty almost came undone.

Hot water rushed over his head, rinsing the shampoo from his hair, down his chest, and sluicing down his legs to disappear down the drain. Rusty grabbed the back of Lucas's head as Lucas continued to suck his cock with an eagerness he couldn't deny.

As his orgasm surfaced, he groaned as he tried to hold it back. Lucas knew exactly how to bring him to the breaking point of a fantastic orgasm within seconds, and holding it in wouldn't be possible for long.

The little sounds coming from his mouth sounded primal. The groans and moans echoing in the steam from the shower came out as sounds he didn't recognize.

His balls drew up close to his groin in preparation for his orgasm. He wouldn't be able to stop it much longer, but when Lucas pushed two fingers into his ass, he lost all control over the rushing tide.

When his orgasm broke over his senses, his whole body shook and shuddered as warmth rushed from his toes to burst through his pelvis like a wave crashing over the ocean shoreline. "Oh my God."

A little Cheshire cat grin spread across Lucas's face as he sat back on his heels and looked up at Rusty. "Very nice, lover. You taste exceptionally good tonight."

Rusty sank down on the small seat built into the wall of the shower as he lost all conscious thought other than what an amazing rush of pleasure he'd felt. "Give me a minute. I need to gather my scattered thoughts."

"No problem, but don't take too long. I'm hard as a rock and I want your ass right here in the shower." He held up the bottle of lube in his hand. "I even brought the lube and a condom."

"Prepared are you?"

"You bet. I couldn't resist that gorgeous body all wet and slick. I had to have a taste and one thing led to another." He grinned again. "Are you complaining?"

"Fuck no. That was fantastic."

"Good, then stand up, bend over, and spread those cheeks for me." Lucas rolled the condom over his cock before slicking it up with the lube. "I want to feel your gorgeous asshole surrounding my aching cock."

Rusty stood, turned around, and bent over, bracing himself on the wall. Lucas got behind him, positioned his cock at Rusty's entrance and then slowly pushed his cock through the muscles.

The feel of all that hardness penetrating him had Rusty's cock stirring to life. Before he knew it, he was hard again and aching to orgasm even though he'd just come so hard, he'd seen stars. "Fuck, Lucas."

"Oh, I know. Believe me, I know what you're feeling. So good. So tight. Fuck, your ass is the best thing I've felt in a long time."

"Harder, please, harder."

Lucas began to fuck him in earnest, ramming his cock into his ass hard and fast. Rusty palmed his cock, working the flesh with his hand up and down, masturbating to the same rhythm Lucas had taken up as he fucked him hard.

"That's it, Rusty, work that gorgeous cock for me. I want to see you paint the wall with your cum."

His breath came out in a hard pant as Lucas continued to fuck him with everything he had. This wasn't a slow, sensual fuck, it was a primal, hard fuck that would leave them both breathless when it was all said and done and just what Rusty needed.

As the dream dissipated from his mind, Rusty realized his cock was hard and wanting. He could almost feel Lucas's cock riding his ass in the shower like he'd done the night before, and now he wanted that again. He needed to feel Lucas ram his cock into his ass hard enough to scoot him across the couch.

It would have to wait though. He had an appointment in a short time, with a potential sponsor, one who could make or break his career with a single word of yes or no.

Chapter Nine

Lucas and Rusty pulled through the gates of the Rocking C in Rusty's truck right on time to meet with the potential sponsor Mr. Campbell had set up. He was thrilled when Lucas had volunteered to drive him out there. The support was a welcome addition. Nerves wracked his body, making his heart race, his breathing rapid and shallow, and his palms sweaty. This could mean the end to his career or the beginning of a beautiful time in his life, and he was scared to death.

The Rocking C was a huge ranch spanning several thousands of acres on the outskirts of Albuquerque. The white ranch house standing off in the distance put his own small place to shame, with its long winding porch wrapped all the way around the front, the manicured gardens off to the left, the huge fenced pastures in front, and the ginormous barn in the distance. Rusty was in awe at the grandeur around him. This was what he wanted someday.

As they pulled up to the front of the house, Mr. Campbell came down the long steps to greet them.

"Rusty. It's great to see you again. How have you been? How's the leg?" he asked after they'd opened the truck's door and stepped out.

"Hi, Mr. Campbell. I'm doin' fine. The leg is all healed and I'm ready to ride when the season starts next week."

"What the hell happened to your face?"

"I got in a bit of a brawl at one of the bars. I'm fine though."

"Glad to hear it. You look pretty banged up. I know that break was a hard one on you, but you've done amazing getting all healed up." Mr. Campbell turned to face Lucas. "You must be Lucas Jacks. I've heard a lot about you on the circuit as well. You are a great up and coming rider. A few more years of experience under your belt, and you'll be in the same league as Rusty."

Lucas frowned as he shook Mr. Campbell's hand. "It's nice to meet you, sir."

Rusty could tell Lucas held back what he really wanted to say. Mr. Campbell's remark was a cut to Lucas since he'd been riding almost as long as Rusty had.

Mr. Campbell slapped Rusty on the back and guided him up the stairs toward the front door of the house. "You must have been practicing recently, Rusty. You look like you got the wrong end of a ride there, son."

"Yeah, I did. I've been out to a riding school outside of town, doing some practice rides."

"I'm sure they aren't as rank as my bulls, but I bet it gave you some good practice."

"Yes, sir, they did. They were very nice out there, letting me get on some of their bulls."

"Very good, but I bet you're ready to ride some of mine."

"Oh yes, sir, I sure am."

"Good, good."

They walked through the front door and Rusty was in awe. The entryway had white marble on the floor with black etchings depicting the Rocking C brand right into the floor. Chandeliers hung from the ceiling and gold accents graced every corner and edge. Rusty was afraid to touch anything least he mar the beautiful furniture.

"Right this way, Rusty. Mr. Coleman is waiting on the back patio next to the pool for us."

Rusty glanced back behind him to make sure Lucas was following. He was although he didn't look happy at all. Rusty knew the feeling. He was totally out of his league here.

As they walked through the double sliding glass doors, Rusty could see a built-in swimming pool off to his left with a rock waterfall at the back where water ran into the pool in a beautiful cascade. Everything was lined with rocks, and native grasses swayed in the breeze. Everywhere he looked was expensive furniture and accents.

When he glanced to his right, he met the brown eyed gaze of Dirk Coleman, owner of Coleman Enterprises and one of the biggest sponsors on the circuit. Rusty had no idea the experienced sponsor Mr. Campbell had mentioned was Coleman Enterprises.

Sitting next to him was a pretty dark-haired girl with the same chocolate gaze as Mr. Coleman. Rusty figured it was Mr. Coleman's daughter. She was pretty enough with her long hair pulled back in a ponytail and her bright-eyed gaze focused on him.

"Dirk Coleman, this is Rusty Arnold. Rusty this is Dirk Coleman and his daughter, Jessica."

"Howdy." Rusty motioned to Lucas. "And this is my friend and fellow rider, Lucas Jacks."

Mr. Coleman stood and held out his hand. "It's nice to meet you, Rusty and Lucas."

"Likewise, Mr. Coleman." Rusty turned to acknowledge Mr. Coleman's daughter. "Jessica."

"I'm a big fan of yours, Rusty," she said, climbing to her feet and holding out her hand. "I've been watching your career for a while now. I was devastated to hear about your injury."

"I appreciate it. It was rough to have to sit out the rest of the season, but I'm ready to climb on those bulls again when the season starts in New York."

"I'm sure you are."

"Please, sit down, y'all. I'll get some drinks for everyone. What would you like?" Mr. Campbell asked as he eyed the group.

"I'll take some water, if you would," Rusty replied as he motioned for Lucas to take a chair beside him. "Lucas?"

"Water is good for me as well."

After Mr. Campbell had taken everyone's order and disappeared into the house to retrieve everything, Rusty turned to Mr. Coleman so he could hopefully get this meeting over with quickly. Not that he minded being in their company, but he really felt out of place. "Mr. Coleman, my understanding is you're interested in possibly becoming a sponsor for me on the circuit?"

"Yes, Rusty, I am. I watched you last year, before your accident, and I think you could easily take the championship next year. Of course, I haven't seen you ride since you broke your leg, but I have every confidence in you and think Coleman Enterprises would look fantastic on the sleeve of your shirt."

"I'm honored, sir."

"Just out of pure curiosity, what happened to your face?"

"I got in a bit of a brawl at the bar last night. Some guy made a pass at someone I was with, and when he was told to take a hike, he didn't like it much. He took a swing at me, connecting with my face, and knocking me to the ground. He got off several punches before I could recover."

"Well, that's too bad. That kind of brings up something we need to discuss if Coleman Enterprises is to be your sponsor. There are some conditions to our sponsorship."

"Conditions?"

"Yes."

"What kind of conditions?"

"It shouldn't be too big of a concern for you, Rusty. You are a clean cut, easygoing kind of young man. The big thing is we don't want any negative publicity." Mr. Coleman laughed. "You know, no getting drunk, no hanging out with prostitutes, keeping your nose clean. Those kinds of things."

Nothing like shooting me down the rabbit hole. If he gets wind of me being gay, this could totally blow up in my face. "I see."

"Also, one more thing. I would love to see you hanging out with Jessica. She could be the pretty little thing on your arm, you know? Every young man needs a beautiful woman to hang out with."

Mr. Coleman winked in his direction and Rusty's stomach sank into the pit of his belly. He knew exactly what the guy meant. He was hoping to play matchmaker with his daughter and Rusty.

Fuck. This could get really ugly fast. Now what the hell do I do?

Rusty glanced at Lucas hoping to see something in his gaze that would help him out of this jam. One of Lucas's eyebrows shot up over his left eye as a frown pulled down the corners of his mouth. *No help there.*

"Listen, Mr. Coleman. I'm not sure if I can meet your conditions."

"Why's that, son?"

"It's not that I tend to get drunk after riding or would cause you any embarrassment on the circuit, but my personal life is my own. I don't see how that would affect you as my sponsor."

Mr. Coleman folded his hands over his paunch that served as his stomach. The man was big enough to need two chairs as the one beneath him groaned in protest. He had a badly receding hairline, brown eyes that looked like the mud hole in Rusty's backyard, jowls that hung down and wiggled as he moved, and chubby legs that looked like they could hardly hold up his weight.

Rusty smiled to himself as he imagined the man trying to pawn off his daughter on some up and coming bull rider. Not that Jessica was ugly because she wasn't, but when a man doesn't have any choice in who he falls in love with, he'd best keep clear of matchmaking sponsors and their daughters.

Jessica winked at him as she titled her head to the side with a come-hither look. She'd probably bedded half the guys on the circuit already, if Rusty was any judge.

A lightbulb went on in his head. He knew he'd seen her before, and yeah, it was behind the chutes in a precarious position with C.B. Parker. Her jeans had been hanging around one ankle, her feet were in the air, and C.B. had been pounding into her. It had been in the corner in the rider's room where they changed clothes and stored their gear during the rides. Come to think of it, he'd seen her hanging around the chutes more times than not last year. Now he knew why. She was the one loose buckle bunny everyone had been with except a select few.

"The big thing is, Rusty, I don't need any bad publicity on the Coleman name. If we were to sponsor you, you would have to keep your nose clean and out of the papers, if you know what I mean."

"I understand, sir. All I can say is I'll do my best."

"All right then." Mr. Coleman held out his hand. "Welcome to the Coleman family, Rusty. I hope we have a long and profitable relationship and with a little luck, a championship belt buckle with a nice healthy check attached at the end of the season."

* * * *

Lucas felt like he wanted to puke. The look on Rusty's face when he'd made the deal with Mr. Coleman was something out of a horror movie for him. His gut tightened and he thought his lunch would come back up by the time they'd made it back to Rusty's place.

He knew exactly what Mr. Coleman wanted from Rusty and it went against everything Rusty wanted for himself. He wanted to come out about his sexual preferences to everyone, but now, he wouldn't be able to. He'd have to keep everything quiet. That was good with Lucas, but he knew Rusty wouldn't be too happy about the change in plans.

"You okay?"

"Yeah, why?"

"Just curious since I know you didn't like the conditions Mr. Coleman put on your association."

"No, I don't, but I need the sponsorship especially for this coming year since it's a comeback year for me." Rusty glanced across the cab of the truck before looking back out the windshield. "Did you recognize Jessica?"

"You mean spread your legs Jessica Coleman? Yep. I remember seeing her around the chutes and the bars we hung out at after the rides. She's been with half, if not more, of the riders on the circuit. I'm surprised her daddy doesn't know."

"I don't know that he doesn't. I wonder if he's trying to hook her up with someone so she'll clean up her act."

"Who knows, but I thought it rather funny he was trying to hook her up with you since you're gay."

"He doesn't know that, and I'm not going to tell him."

"What if it gets leaked to the papers? He'll pull his sponsorship in a heartbeat."

"I know."

"So what are you going to do?"

Rusty shrugged as he continued to ponder his predicament. Now that his dad knew about him, he probably wasn't sure what to do. For now he had to keep his sponsor happy even if it meant keeping their relationship a secret. "Keep quiet, I guess. I need his money and his name."

"I know this sticks in your craw, Rusty, but I think it's for the best."

"I knew you would. You don't want it out anyway."

"It's not so much that anymore. It's more like it's my business what I do on my off time and no one else's, but being in the public eye like we are, it's difficult to keep our private lives private." Lucas stroked his stubbled chin in thought. He knew what he wanted and he knew what Rusty wanted, but everything had gone to hell in a handbasket in the last twelve hours. Again, they would have to keep what they did behind closed doors to themselves and hope to hell Rusty's family didn't blast it all over the media.

"Are you going to tell your parents?"

"Hell no. Mine would be worse than yours. Neither of my parents would understand. My sister Sheryl is supportive, but my brother, Ethan, would never get it."

"I'm sorry."

"Don't be. It's something I have to live with and at least I know up front they are homophobic. I don't have any delusions they would support me."

"This whole thing is fucked up."

"Don't I know it."

They pulled up to Rusty's house a few minutes later. Lucas saw Rusty's face blanch when he recognized Russell's truck in his driveway. When they both stepped out, Russell met them at the front hood of the truck.

"Why are you here, Russell?"

"I came to see my big brother." Russell swayed on his feet. *Great. The motherfucker was drunk.*

"You only come over here when you want something, so what is it?"

"Dad told me you're a queer. I want to know the truth."

"If you mean am I gay, yes, I am."

"Well now, isn't that just fucking peachy. My macho, bull riding big brother is a fucking faggot."

"You can leave anytime, Russell."

"I'll leave when I'm damned good and ready, queerbait. I have a few things to say to you."

"What might that be?"

"You've always held it over my head that you were born fifteen minutes before me and that you were the favorite of us boys. Not anymore. Dad hates you. He cursed you this morning for several hours, calling you all kinds of names, and I'm here to tell you that you are no longer welcome in our family. You might as well change your name because Arnold doesn't belong to you anymore. Dad and Mom have disowned you."

Rusty got right up in Russell's face to where their noses almost touched. Looking at the two of them like this made Lucas realized even though they shared the womb, they were two very different individuals.

"You can go straight to hell, Russell. I've talked to Mom and she supports me as do the boys. I get Dad can't deal with this. He'll get over it eventually, and no, I won't be stepping on Arnold property until he calms down, but I'm telling you this, my name is still Arnold and I will proudly carry that name to my deathbed. I am still your brother and I'm still his son whether you like it or not. What I do behind closed doors in my own home is no one's business but mine and my partner's."

"You'd better get your PR people ready to shush it up because I plan to smear you all over the media."

"You do your worst, Russell. I'm not afraid of you."

"You should be. I plan to grind you into the ground and piss on you as you hit the dirt."

"Get off my land before I do something I will regret because you are my brother."

Russell didn't respond. He stepped back, glared at Rusty one last time, and then headed to his truck. Lucas could see that even though Russell worked cattle for a living, Rusty had him in muscle bulk. Rusty wasn't a slouch by any stretch of the imagination, and Lucas wasn't so sure who would win a brawl between the brothers.

Gravel sprayed both of them as Russell took off down the driveway as fast as he could without putting himself in the ditch.

Rusty stood staring after his brother with his hands balled into fists, his breathing coming out in rapid pants, and his body shaking with rage.

"You okay?" Lucas asked, stopping at Rusty's side.

"No."

"What can I do to help?"

"Find me a bull to ride. I need to work off this useless rage I'm feeling right now."

"How about calling the riding school and see if we can go out there for a few hours?"

Rusty nodded and Lucas pulled out his phone to call.

Within a few minutes, they were back on the road. He told Rusty he would drive again as he shoved him into the passenger seat of the truck, and headed out for the Double L. He didn't think it was a good idea for Rusty to be driving when he was this angry.

They didn't talk the entire ride, but he could tell Rusty was still fuming by the red streaks on his cheeks, his fisted hands, and the relentless tapping of his boot on the floorboard. Lucas hoped this school had a couple of rank bulls because Rusty needed to vent and only a bull that would buck hard would do.

As they pulled through the double wrought iron gates of the Double L, Lucas was surprised to see a pretty nice setup. The place was good sized, had a nice arena, and a pretty big barn. Logan Tyler stood near the fence waiting for them to park.

"Hi there."

"Mr. Tyler," Rusty replied.

"I thought we were friends, Rusty. It's Logan to you." He held out his hand to Lucas. "You must be Lucas Jacks. I've heard a lot about you too."

"It's nice to meet you, sir."

"Please, call me Logan."

"All right, Logan." Lucas exhaled. "Listen, Logan, Rusty's had a pretty rough day, and could really use a hard ride to work off some anger."

"You okay, Rusty?"

"Yeah. I just had a bad run-in with my father and my twin brother today."

"I can tell by the bruises on your face, you probably got the raw end of the deal there."

"I didn't swing back, if that's what you mean."

"Your dad?"

"Yeah."

"Well then, let me see who I have in the barn that might work for you. I've got a couple of young bulls that are bucking pretty good. I think they might give you a bit of a challenge." He turned to head toward the barn. "Follow me, boys, and we'll see what we can do."

As they disappeared into the cooler interior of the huge white barn, Lucas noticed the numerous paddocks lining the walkway. Most had nameplates on the stalls to indicate where one of the animals belonged. He didn't know if Logan Tyler only bred bulls or other livestock as well.

"You've never been here, Lucas, so let me show you around a bit." They continued to walk as Logan pointed out the stalls. "These are where my horses are kept. I breed bucking broncs for the rodeo as well as bulls for the pro bull rider's circuit. My son takes the horses to most of the rodeos while I do the bulls."

"Wow." Lucas was impressed with whole layout. Logan had a great setup, one that Lucas could see going somewhere someday soon.

"It's a big operation and one I'm very proud of, although I hope some of my bulls make it into the pro circuit soon. Right now, we are only working some of the smaller venues on the circuit. You know, the semi-pros so to speak."

"Yes, sir."

"Have you boys ever done rodeo rides?"

"Yes, we have," Rusty answered. "We were both youth riders in high school on both horses and bulls."

"Then you will be impressed with our arena. Rusty, you've already seen it up close and personal, but Lucas hasn't." Mr. Taylor led the way toward the walkway that led out into the fenced arena.

Lucas whistled softly. The enclosure was massive in size with fencing going all the way around. He also had spectator seats on two sides where he could host a riding competition or junior rodeo himself right here on his property. "Nice."

"I'd like to ask you two a favor, if I may. I know you are both active riders on the pro circuit, but as you know, I have a youth group here of potential riders who could use some pointers from the pros. They aren't here today, but I would be very honored if you two could make time to come by one day and help them. I've been a rodeo rider all my life, but bulls are not my specialty to ride. I breed them, yes, but ride them, no. It would be fantastic if they could get a few pointers from a couple of pros."

"I would be honored," Rusty replied. "After all, you are doing us a huge favor by letting us practice on your bulls."

Logan kicked at a dirt clod under his boot. "I'll admit there was an ulterior motive to me letting you boys ride. I'm hoping you can help me out by recommending us as a contractor next year on some of the stops."

"If your bulls are as good as you say they are, I would be more than happy to recommend you," Lucas answered, taking a bit of the focus off Rusty for the moment. Not that Rusty didn't deserve it and more, but he was a rider too, and a damned good one. Rusty glanced his way, but he just grinned.

"Fantastic. Rusty?"

"I'd be happy to recommend you as well. I know your bulls have the potential to be a challenge for the riders on the circuit."

"Great. Let me get my boys to set up a few in the chutes over there. You two brought your bull ropes, right?"

"Never leave home without it." Lucas stepped toward where the chutes were located and looked around. The setup was pretty damned close to what the professionals did during a stop on the circuit. Big iron gates encircled the entire arena with a couple of chutes set up on this end for them to herd the bulls in for a ride. It looked like a top-notch facility and one he couldn't wait to ride in. "Do you have a couple of guys to be wranglers?"

"Yep. If you two will grab your ropes, get them ready, and suit up, we will corral two of our best bulls into the chutes and see what you've got."

Lucas grinned and smacked Rusty on the shoulder. "Let's get our stuff." As they headed back out to where Lucas had parked the truck, Rusty frowned. "What's up?"

"I'm in a really pissy mood, I guess. I hope I can ride. I really need to let some of this anger go, otherwise, I'll give myself an ulcer or something."

"It'll be okay, Rusty."

"I hope Mr. Tyler has more than two bulls for us to ride. I wouldn't want to wear them out because I really need to ride more than once."

"I know what you mean, but I'm sure he can accommodate us, especially if he wants us to endorse his bulls for the circuit."

"That's another thing. Are you sure you're okay with that?"

"Why not? If they are good bulls, I can't see why it would be a problem." Lucas opened the truck, grabbed his rope and Rusty's before shutting it again. "Besides, it's not like the circuit will really listen to us anyway, right?"

"I don't want to give him hope if there isn't a chance it would help."

"Let's see how the rides go. Then we'll worry about whether to endorse him or not."

Rusty nodded as they walked back toward the barn.

Lucas figured it would be good for them either way to endorse the bulls and the riding school. They might end up with a sponsorship named after them out of the deal. That sure wouldn't hurt his feelings, plus if Rusty got another sponsor who didn't care about their sexual orientation, then he could tell Mr. Coleman to stick his conditions up his ass.

Chapter Ten

Rusty eased himself down on the bull's back as Lucas wrapped his rope around its belly, stretching the end up to tie it tight around his middle. After he'd secured his riding hand, he scooted up so he was centered on the animal's back and nodded quickly for the gateman to open the panel.

Time stopped as the bull spun to the left, leapt straight up, and then spun to the right, his legs kicking out behind him with every twist of his body or change in his position. Rusty hung on with his right hand while holding his left hand above his head. His thighs screamed from the pressure. His back ached from the snap of the bull as it moved. His whole body burned from the movement.

He'd never felt more alive than he did right then, eight seconds of pure adrenaline rush. He lived for these moments, for those few seconds on the back of several thousand pounds of muscle that could break a man in half.

When the air horn blew, he reached down, untied his hand and careened off the side of the animal before scrambling toward the metal rail fencing surrounding the arena.

Lucas raised a fist, pumping it in the air in celebration for what probably would have been a ninety point ride. "That was fantastic, Rusty!"

"Thanks. It felt good."

"How is your leg feeling?"

"Fine. Not even sore with that one. Of course, I probably will be tomorrow when the rush wears off."

"True, buddy, very true."

"How did it look from your point of view?"

"It was a great ride. You were centered, you were over the bull's front legs, you kept your balance, your arm was well above your head so there was no chance of touching. It looked awesome."

Rusty slapped the dirt off his chaps after he'd jumped over the railing onto the other side. He felt good, fantastic even. He was ready to ride come January. He knew it now. Everything had fit into place just like he'd never left.

"Wow." Logan stopped next to him and slapped him on the back. "I can certainly see why you were reigning champion last year. That was one of the best rides I've ever seen."

"Thanks. It felt good."

"You remind me of Lane Frost, you know. He was one of the best riders on the circuit when he was killed. I got to see him ride once, when I was a teenager. He made it look so easy, just like you do."

"I appreciate the support, Logan." He glanced up to Lucas. "You ready for your turn?"

"Hell yeah. I haven't been on a bull in weeks. I'm feeling deprived."

Rusty shook his head and laughed as he helped Lucas position the rope.

When Lucas got himself settled, rope in place, Rusty watched from the sidelines as Lucas nodded and the gate burst open.

The bull wasn't quite as active as the one Rusty had, but it was another good bull, one that would certainly do for the pro circuit, if they could get Double L bulls out there.

An idea flashed into Rusty's mind. What if he could become a sponsor of the bucking bulls the Double L had, while the Double L became one of his sponsors? Would Logan go for that? He wasn't sure, but it sounded like it might be a great plan for both of them.

The idea had merit, but for now, he would talk to Lucas and see what he said about it. Since they were both riders on the circuit, they could put a bug in the ear of the head of the contractors to see about getting the Double L bulls in. He hoped it wouldn't be a conflict of interest on their parts though. If the judges found out he was a sponsor of the bucking bulls and it was one of their bulls he rode one night, he could be disqualified. He and Lucas would have to make doubly sure none of the Double L bulls were competing when they were riding. *Hmm. This is something I'm going to have to think over seriously before I say anything to Logan.*

After Lucas's eight second buzzer sounded, he leapt from the back of the bull cleanly and smoothly before making a run for the railing. As he flipped himself over the rail, landing on the other side on his feet, he grinned like a cat that ate the canary.

"That was great, Lucas. Easily and eighty eight point ride if not more."

"The bull didn't buck quite as much as yours. The one you had was a spinner and would have gotten a better score, but mine was turning right into my hand. He made it look easy to get a good score."

"Take what you can get."

Logan appeared around the side of the chute with a big grin on his face. "You both did fantastic. I can certainly see why you two are some of the best riders on the circuit."

Excitement had red streaks splashing across Lucas's face. His breathing was fast and Rusty could see his heartbeat pounding in his neck. "Do you have a few more we can get on?"

"Yes, I do. I would love for you two to evaluate all the bulls I have currently in line for a contractor's position. It would help me tremendously for you two to ride them so you can see what they do that is good and what they might have points counted off for."

Rusty nodded his understanding. "Certainly, Logan. We would love to and this helps us out a lot too. We've been slacking some during this break and with the tours starting up again in a week, we need to get into shape."

"Good. Let's get a couple more ready in the chutes." Logan moved toward the left to talk to his guys as Rusty and Lucas readied their ropes.

"Are you sure you're all right? You don't want to hurt yourself again before the season starts."

"I'm fine, Lucas. I feel really good, and I'm ready to go."

"Great. I was worried, is all."

"I know and I appreciate it, but I'll be okay. I needed this."

Nodding, Lucas put his hand on Rusty's shoulder and squeezed a little to let Rusty know he cared without being too obvious with Logan around. They could celebrate better once they were done here, but for now they had to keep things on the down low.

For the rest of the afternoon, Lucas and Rusty rode every bull Logan could throw at them. Some they did eight seconds on, some they didn't, but when all was said and done, it was a fantastic afternoon and one Rusty wouldn't forget anytime soon. "Logan, you have no idea how much we appreciate you letting us on your bulls."

"You've done me much more of a favor than I've done for you two. These bulls needed the workout and it helped me tremendously to see pros ride them so I can see what I need to work on with them to get them ready. I appreciate you two taking the time over here."

"It's been our pleasure."

"Can I interest you two into staying for supper? My wife makes a mean meatloaf."

"If it wouldn't be too much trouble, we'd love to."

"No trouble at all. She always makes way too much anyway so two more mouths to feed would be her pleasure, trust me."

They laughed as they headed down the walkway toward the main part of the barn. His guys had put the bulls away, fed them, and watered them, so each one munched happily in their stalls as they walked back toward the big doors that led outside. When they reached the end, they flipped off the lights before turning toward the house in the distance.

As they approached the house, Logan's wife came out with an apron tied around her waist, her hair up in a tight little bun at the back of her head, pretty floral dress on, and a smile on her face. "I hope you two are joining us for supper."

"We'd be happy too, Mrs. Tyler."

"Please call me Marie. I think of my mother-in-law when someone calls me Mrs. Tyler."

"Pleasure to, ma'am."

They followed her into the house and Rusty was struck by the homey atmosphere she had created in decorating their home. A large leather sofa stood off to the left with a beautiful wooden sofa table in front of it. Two leather arm chairs sat across the room with all of them facing the large television on the wall. Indian weave rugs covered the wooden floor and from what Rusty could see of it, they were a gorgeous walnut.

"This way, gentleman. The dining room table has plenty of room for everyone. I just need to grab a couple more plates and glasses from the cupboard."

When they rounded the corner, Rusty was in awe of the large table with several chairs on each side of it that took up most of the room. They obviously liked to entertain or they fed a lot of people at once. "Wow. What a beautiful table."

"It belonged to Logan's grandfather. He used to run a large cattle ranch in Texas and he had this in his bunk house to feed all the hands. We have a big family, so it was a fantastic find for us to put in our home. We always have large get-togethers." She motioned for them to take a seat at one end. "You boys take any chair. I'll get the food served up."

"Is there anything I can do to help?" Rusty asked, remembering the gatherings at home when his mom fed all of them at once. It was a chore to say the least.

"You're company. You sit."

"Yes, ma'am."

The all took seats surrounding one end of the table and sat quietly until Marie came back in, set the table, and handed them all a beer.

"I'm sure you boys need something cold and wet since you've been riding all day. Enjoy your beer while I get the food on the table."

Rusty tipped the bottle to his lips, enjoying the wash of malty liquid that slid down his throat. He sighed as it hit his empty stomach. *Man, that hit the spot.* He glanced at Lucas who was enjoying his beer, too. One wouldn't hurt, but neither of them could have anymore before they had to leave since they had a bit of a drive to get home.

Marie returned a few minutes later with plates piled high with meatloaf, mashed potatoes, corn on the cob, and rolls for everyone. "Eat up. You are growing boys. You need your strength to wrangle those bulls."

The food tasted fantastic. The meatloaf was perfect with a smoky flavor that his taste buds enjoyed tremendously, the potatoes were ideal, creamy with just the right amount of gravy, and the corn had to have been right out of the garden he'd seen around back of the house. "This is awesome, Marie. You are one great cook."

"Well, thank you, Rusty. I've had a bit of practice over the last thirty years since Logan and I got married and raised our kids." She took a sip of wine from her glass. "Do you have a big family?"

"Yes, ma'am. I have a twin brother and three other brothers."

"Very good. I like big families. What about you, Lucas?"

"Just one brother and one sister."

"Three isn't bad either. Logan and I have six children all together. Most of them are on their own now, but our youngest son helps around here with the horses."

"I do believe I met your daughter the first time I came out, and Logan mentioned your son takes the horses to rodeos."

"Yes, he does. I'm hoping he'll settle down with someone pretty soon." She glanced at Logan and then back to Rusty. "He's gay so it makes it even more difficult for him to find the one person he's meant to be with."

Rusty choked on his beer.

"Not that it would make a lot of difference to some people, but others aren't so forgiving of anyone who is different."

"True." Rusty took another bite of his food. The information that their youngest son was gay sent Rusty's thought careening. They obviously were okay with it and even supported their son in his lifestyle. *What a difference between Logan and Marie and my dad's reaction to my news.*

"I guess since you and Lucas might be helping to promote Double L Bucking Bulls on the circuit, I should have told you about Aiden."

"It's okay, Logan. We don't have a problem with it."

Logan sighed in relief. "Thank you. It means a lot to me to know you two aren't freaked out by him being gay. His mother and I fully support him. To us, he's still our son no matter who he chooses to fall in love with."

"Lucas and I have friends on the circuit who are gay and in a committed relationship. It doesn't bother us at all."

"That's good to know."

The rest of the meal consisted of lively conversation about the bulls Logan wanted to try to get on the circuit and what Lucas and Rusty could do to help. Rusty felt more and more that it was meant to be for them to be part of the Double L Bucking Bulls on a long term basis.

When he and Lucas headed home later that evening, he quietly contemplated how to bring up the subject to Lucas without making him feel left out of the entire thought process.

"You're very quiet."

"I'm thinking."

"About?"

"This afternoon."

"And?"

"What would you say about us going into business with Logan?"

"How so?"

"I mean the bucking bulls part of his operation. I'm thinking we could be silent partners, investing in the breeding program he has going, and helping him get a contract with the pro circuit to bring his bulls to the tour."

"You know that having us involved in everything might cause a conflict of interest."

"I know. I don't know about you and how you are feeling about your career at the moment, but I'm thinking long term here. We aren't going to be able to ride bulls forever. Most riders retire at thirty-five or less."

"Yes, they do because most are so broken by falls, spills, and injuries that they can't continue."

"True, but wouldn't you like to have something to fall back on when the time comes? It would be great to continue to be a part of the circuit even after we stop riding."

Lucas stroked his chin in contemplation before he said, "I can see where you're coming from and I totally agree with you. One thing though, we would have to talk to the commissioners of the circuit to get their take on our involvement in Logan's business and how that might affect our riding."

"Logan's bulls won't be ready for the circuit for a couple of years if what I saw today was any indication. They bucked well, but they're still a bit young."

"I agree."

"Good, then we can call and talk to Logan tomorrow to see what he thinks of the idea."

"Sounds good to me."

When they drove through the gates of home, Rusty wondered what the rest of the evening might bring. He was hoping Lucas would stay again tonight, but he wasn't going to hold his breath for it. Lucas had to teach in the morning and when he did that, he normally didn't stay at Rusty's. His bed would be cold and lonely tonight.

The lights of his house were like a beacon welcoming them home, until he got closer and realized some shit had went down while they'd been gone.

The front windows were broken, the door hung off the hinges, and the front yard looked like someone had taken a four-wheeler and tore up the grass. "What the fuck?"

"Holy shit!"

Rusty threw the truck into park, turned off the key and jumped out. "Oh my God. Who would do something like this?"

QUEER was written in big red letters across his door.

"I'm going to fucking kill him!"

"Who do you think did this?"

"It had to be Russell. He's asshole enough to do something like this, thinking he's a big man, while out to hurt me in the process." Rusty sank down on the front steps. "Does he hate me that much, Lucas? I'm his brother, his twin."

"I know, Rusty, but he's probably afraid right now, terrified that someone will find out about you and it will reflect on him. He's not gay and he can't understand how you can be if you two shared the same womb."

"We aren't identical though."

"No, you aren't, and believe me, I can totally see the differences between you in personality and everything. He's always been a bit of a jerk, even in high school."

"Yeah, I remember him picking on people that were smaller than he was. He's always been a bit of a bully."

"Right, and now he's taking it out on you."

Rusty got to his feet and stepped up on the porch so he could see the damage inside the house.

When he walked inside, he wasn't surprised to see the overturned furniture, the broken lamps, and the crushed family pictures from his mantel. If Russell had done this, he definitely did it as a means to hurt him.

Lucas grabbed a broom from the kitchen and began to clean up the glass.

Nick came skidding through the front door, shock written on his face. "What happened here? It looks like a bomb went off."

"Someone broke in while Lucas and I were gone, tore things up and broke a bunch of stuff."

"Do you have any idea who it might have been?"

"Lucas thinks it was Russell."

"Why do you think that?"

"Because today my father and the rest of my family found out I'm gay."

"You told them?"

"Yeah."

"Is that why your face is tore up too?"

Rusty nodded. "Courtesy of my father."

"Holy shit."

"Can you get some plywood from the barn, Nick, and help me nail some up over the windows for now? I'll go into town tomorrow and get some new ones."

"You'll need a new door, too. That one has been ripped off the hinges."

"I know. Most of the damage is minor though."

"What are you going to do about this? You can't lie back and let them bully you like this, Rusty. This is bullshit." The fierceness on Nick's face surprised Rusty. He knew Nick was loyal to him as an employee, but having him on his side when shit went down was kind of different. Of course, with Nick having gay tendencies too, that might be why. He might feel that this was a mark against him too, as well as Lucas.

"I don't plan to take it lying down, Nick. I will confront my brother tomorrow after I've had a chance to cool off."

"Good." Nick took a step back toward the door. "I'll go get the plywood."

"Thanks."

Lucas continued to sweep up the debris on the floor into a pile, and then put it in the dustpan he'd found in the kitchen. Rusty grabbed the pictures from the floor, putting them back on the mantel where they belonged even though the glass had been broken.

The smiling faces of his parents stared back from one, while another was of him and Russell as young boys, each holding a fishing pole in one hand while a large trout dangled from the line. They'd been so close once, but now it seemed like so long ago.

His father hated him. His brother hated him. His mother was torn by the rift now growing larger and larger between them. Who knew how his younger brothers felt? He needed to talk to them and soon.

All because of who he chose to have sex with.

When he glanced across the room to where Lucas continued to right the furniture, he began to realize that no matter what, Lucas would be by his side at least as a friend.

Could he convince his lover that they could build a future together as a family?

Love just might win out in the end if he was careful.

Slow and easy.

Chapter Eleven

New York City in January. It was a beautiful place with the snow piled high, but Rusty didn't care for it. Luckily, they were only there for a few days.

Rusty and Lucas had been to The Big Apple before, but the noise, the lights, and the craziness always seemed overwhelming to the country boy Rusty had grown up as.

The cab pulled up in front of the hotel where they would be staying for the rides this weekend. Paparazzi hung out in front waiting for the riders to arrive. This was opening weekend for the pro bull rider's circuit for the 2016 season.

Christmas had been interesting at his house. Lucas almost lived there these days, but Rusty wasn't putting a name on what was going on between them. They shared Christmas dinner with the hands on his place, exchanged small gifts that weren't personal in nature, and had great sex. Rusty didn't know what to make of the small changes in their relationship. Going with the flow seemed to be what they were going to do for now.

His father and Russell hadn't made his business known throughout Albuquerque, so for that he was thankful. So far, there had been no more attacks on his property. When he had contacted the police about the vandalism, there wasn't much they could do except take a report since no one had seen Russell do it. Even if he would have been seen on the property, it wouldn't have been odd to anyone that he was there.

Mr. Coleman did his part on the sponsorship even though he was continually pushing Jessica toward Rusty by making suggestions about them being seen together. So far, Rusty had been able to avoid being seen with her. Now that the circuit had started again, that might not be so easy.

Logan Tyler had come through with a sponsorship for both Rusty and Lucas. It was smaller than what he would receive from Coleman Enterprises, but Rusty felt a lot better about Double L sponsoring him than he did about Coleman Enterprises.

For now, he and Lucas kept their support of Double L Bucking Bulls quiet. Logan didn't have any bulls on the pro circuit yet, so he didn't think there would be a problem with a conflict of interest. When and if the time came, he would talk to the commissioner of the circuit to get that squared away.

When the door to the cab opened, Rusty stepped out to flashing cameras, yelling reporters, and fans galore. There had to be over a hundred people waiting for him.

"Rusty, are you ready for 2016?"

"Yes I am. I feel great."

"How did you spend your time off from the circuit since last October?"

"I got to work out on some barrels and even rode some great up and coming bulls. You should expect to see some really talented animals coming out of the Double L Bucking Bulls."

"You and Lucas Jacks are good friends. Did he help you on your downtime?"

"Yes. Lucas and I have been friends since high school. His advice on my form during our practice runs, helped tremendously."

"I heard you snagged a lucrative sponsorship with Coleman Enterprises and that you are seeing Mr. Coleman's daughter, Jessica."

"I do have a new sponsorship from Coleman Enterprises, yes, but my personal life is none of anyone's business." Rusty nodded to the crowd and made his way to the door that led into the hotel. The bellman kept everyone out but those who were supposed to be there. Lucas followed in his footsteps. "Sorry. I know that probably bugged the hell out of you."

"Why?"

"I didn't hear one person ask anything about you or what you were doing on the off season."

"No, but it's fine. You are the comeback hero of 2016, so yeah, they are going to be all about what you did and how you are preparing for the coming season. You are the golden boy this year. It's going to be a difficult thing to live up to."

They walked through the lobby and up to the check-in desk to their right. After they gave Rusty's name, they were handed key cards for their room, grabbed their gear bags from the floor where they'd set them when they stopped at the desk, and headed for the elevator behind the bar.

Rusty glanced to the left, noticing several riders hanging in the leather seated lounge area. He lifted his hand in greeting and noticed some of the guys returning the wave as they called out his name. It was great to be back!

The elevator doors *wooshed* open on the eighth floor to a glass-filled entryway. When they stepped out, they were taken aback by the grandeur of the hotel. They'd never stayed in this one before, so the whole thing was new to them, one of the perks of having Coleman Enterprises as a sponsor.

They went left after they glanced at the numbers on the wall indicating which way their room was. Coleman had set Rusty up with a suite and he figured the best thing for them to do was share a room since neither of them had to pay for it.

After Rusty slid his card into the lock on the door, he pushed it open and was surprised at the luxury of the room. "Wow. This is awesome!" He dropped his gear bag on the floor near the couch and proceeded to check out the place. A full bar sat off to the right as he walked toward what appeared to be a bedroom. The living space was bigger than his at home. Leather couches sat in front of a gas fireplace, black tables accentuated the furniture, all with the large glass windows that would look out over the lights of the city, behind them. Rusty moved toward the bedroom and pushed the door open. A huge king-sized bed took up most of the room. He could totally see him and Lucas fucking on that bed.

To his right was another door. He pushed it open only to find a huge bathroom with a glass enclosed shower large enough for at least two people if not more. It had a great rain type showerhead and several other water spouts on the walls to give you a great massage during your shower.

Lucas came up behind him, sliding his hands around Rusty's middle. "Imagining us in there?"

"Yep."

"Good. Me too."

Lucas kissed him on the neck, right behind his ear. It was a sensitive spot for him and Lucas knew it. Only a touch there could catapult him straight into rock hard.

Rusty turned in his arms to look straight into his fiery blue eyes. Desire raged in his look as he took in every inch of Rusty's face.

"I need you."

"Do you now?"

"Yes. Bad. I want to plunge into your ass so hard, you scoot across the bed with each thrust."

"Um. I could go for that."

"Good. Strip."

Rusty tossed his hat onto the dresser next to the wall before grabbing the button at his waist to turn it loose. Lucas sat on the bed, his cock a hard outline under his jeans. Moisture pooled in Rusty's mouth as he stripped off his clothes with Lucas watching, his gaze focused on the movement of his hands.

As he worked the zipper down on the front of his jeans very slowly, Lucas licked his lips. He loved teasing Lucas with slow peeks of his skin as he undressed. It made them both explosively hot for each other when they did finally get to the fucking part.

Rusty pushed his jeans and boxers to the floor inch by inch, revealing his solid cock to his lover. He toed off his boots before extraditing himself from the worn denim.

Lucas reached for him, but he stepped back with a grin. He wouldn't let Lucas touch him just yet. Anticipation could be vicious when you were that horny, but the rewards would be like being consumed by a raging wildfire. Pre-cum glistened on the tip of his cock. Desire simmered in his blood, making him shiver in expectation of the coming activities.

When he pulled his t-shirt off and over his head, he walked toward Lucas one small step at a time. "Do you want this in your mouth?" he asked, holding his cock and slowly stroking the hard flesh for a few seconds.

"Holy fuck, yes."

"On your knees."

Lucas slid off the bed to where he was positioned on his knees in front of Rusty. Man, did he love to see Lucas in this position. "Put your hands behind your back and keep them there. Don't touch me with anything besides your mouth and tongue." Rusty moved forward a few steps so he could position his cock at Lucas's lips.

When Lucas licked him from balls to tip, Rusty moaned softly and closed his eyes. Warmth engulfed his cock as Lucas took the whole thing between his lips, clear to the base. Lucas stayed still, letting Rusty's cock fuck him in the mouth, until Rusty was ready to cry out for him to stop. He didn't though, just rode the sensations bombarding him. It felt absolutely fabulous to have Lucas sucking his dick.

Lucas let the cock pop from his mouth as he traced the veins running the length of the hard flesh with his tongue. Next, he moved farther down, taking Rusty's balls and sucking each one in turn until Rusty thought his head would detonate.

At the exact moment, Rusty thought he would lose the miniscule amount of control he had on his orgasm. Lucas wet a finger and shoved it knuckle deep into Rusty's ass while at the same time taking Rusty's entire cock into his mouth.

Rusty lost it. Cum shot out the end of his dick straight down Lucas's throat as Lucas hummed his appreciation. His legs shook as he lost control of his body for that split second of satisfaction that always comes with a healthy orgasm. Now overly sensitive, Rusty pulled his softening cock from Lucas's mouth as his lover sat back with a pleased grin on his face.

"I do love when you come in my mouth."

"That was amazing."

"Um, yes it was, but now I'm so hard, I hurt." Lucas climbed to his feet and began to remove his clothes in quick secession. "I'm going to plunder your ass, Rusty."

"Good. I need you to fuck me hard."

Rusty positioned himself over the edge of the bed, his feet spread wide, and his ass in the air. When the cool liquid of the lubrication jelly hit his hole, he jumped before easing back into the sensations he knew were to come. Having Lucas as his lover made him feel loved and accepted even if they hadn't declared any deep feelings for each other. Rusty knew it was a matter of time.

* * * *

Lucas positioned his cock at Rusty's back entrance, easing the hard flesh into his lover's back hole. The slick entrance enveloped him in warmth and wetness, driving his desire to explosive. "You feel fucking amazing."

"Push harder."

"I want to make this last."

"We can fuck again later. Do it."

Lucas pushed all the way in until he was balls deep. When he slowly pulled his cock back out, he had to tamp down his rushing orgasm before he lost it. He wasn't ready to come yet. He wanted to make this last longer than a few minutes.

"Fuck me harder, Lucas."

He wouldn't hold back much longer. Thrust after thrust drove his cock deep. Silky slickness wrapped around his cock. Desire clawed at his insides as his balls drew up against his groin in preparation for his orgasm. "I can't hold back."

"Come in my ass, Lucas. Ram that cock into me."

Lucas's thrusts increased in tempo and fierceness as he did his best to make Rusty enjoy this, too.

When his climax hit, his whole world narrowed to the sensations he was experiencing in his groin. "Oh fuck!" He continued to thrust until he couldn't feel his legs anymore and collapsed onto Rusty's back. His breaths came out in shuddering pants, his heart hammered inside his chest, and his legs shook with fatigue as he waited for his body systems to return to normal.

Rusty lay like a blob under him, so he moved his weight to the side and threw his arm over his eyes. "You okay?"

"Yeah. That was awesome."

"You didn't come again."

"No, but it was still amazing. I came so hard the first time, I didn't think I would even be able to get it up again. I totally enjoyed the fucking though."

"Rusty?"

"Yeah?"

"I think I'm falling in love with you." *What the hell made me say that? Holy shit!*

"You what?"

"Uh. Never mind."

"You can't say shit like that and then say never mind, Lucas."

"It was the sex talking. I didn't mean it."

Rusty leaned over him and slapped his arm away from his face. "Say that to my face, Lucas."

He glanced away, not able to meet Rusty's gaze. He knew in his heart it was true. Could Rusty love him back? Could they build some kind of life together or would they be at odds about their sexuality for the rest of their lives. They couldn't agree on whether to be out and proud or hide their feelings behind closed doors. How could they come to some agreement about how they would live?

Lucas sighed as he turned back toward Rusty. He'd come to love him like a man should love someone they wanted to spend the rest of their life with. Over the last several months, they'd become almost domestic in their relationship. Hell, he spent more time at Rusty's than he did at home these days and now that the circuit had started again, they would be spending more time together than ever while they shared their room and traveled together.

When he looked deep into Rusty's green eyes, he could see something he hadn't wanted to put a name to for the last few weeks. Now he knew what it was, it was love staring back at him.

"I think I'm falling in love with you, Rusty. I think you feel the same about me, but I need to hear you say it because this craziness I'm feeling can't be ignored anymore."

Rusty laughed as he straddled Lucas's hips and sat on him. "You stupid asshole!"

"I don't get it."

"I've been in love with you for so long, I can't remember a time when I wasn't in love with you. I knew you weren't ready to explore a relationship with me, so I kept quiet, but now that I know you are thinking the same way, we can start to move on and build a life together."

"Whoa, Rusty. Slow down." He pushed Rusty's shoulder, dislodging him from his seat on his belly. "We need to think things through. We can't go jumping into something without talking about this."

"What is there to talk about, Lucas? I love you, you love me. You can move into my place when we get back."

"Slow down, slugger."

"Why? Are you still having problems with people knowing we are gay?"

"Yeah. What will happen to your sponsorship with Coleman? We can't discount the kind of money he's supplying." He waved a hand indicating the room around them. "Look at this room. There is no way we can afford this kind of stuff on what we make riding."

Rusty got up from the side of the bed and walked over to where his clothes were in a pile on the floor. He grabbed his jeans, slipped them on without underwear, and buttoned them at the waist. *Thank God. It was difficult enough thinking clearly without that cock rubbing on mine.*

"I know what you mean, Lucas. I understand that a relationship between us will not be easy with everything, but keeping a secret isn't right either." Rusty sat in the armchair on the other side of the room. "I don't want to keep us a secret. I want to shout it to the world."

"I understand, Rusty, I do." He sat up and reached for his clothes as well. Talking was good, being naked while doing it wasn't. "I'm glad we have each other and that we care about each other like that. It seems right to me now that we've said it out loud, but we have to worry about our careers too. You and I both know Coleman won't be happy about the publicity. Logan Tyler won't care, I don't believe. Your father doesn't like the idea and neither does Russell, so you have that to contend with. My parents don't know, at least not yet, but I can tell you there won't be any support there either."

Rusty shoved his fingers through his hair, frustration evident in his movements. Lucas wanted nothing more than to pull him into his embrace, dive beneath the covers, and love away the night. They couldn't though. They had appearances to make.

He glanced at the clock on the nightstand. Five-thirty. They had just about enough time to get some food before they had to be at the meet and greet for the riders in the lobby downstairs.

Interesting note though. He knew Levi and Curt would be here so it would be fascinating to see how the media reacted toward them and their relationship. Lucas knew a few riders on the circuit were gay, but several of them weren't and didn't tolerate gays very well.

"Let's go get some food. I'm starving after that romp and then we can get ready for the meet and greet."

"All right." Rusty got to his feet and headed for the door. "I'll grab your gear bag and suitcase."

Lucas grabbed a glass of water from the bathroom while he waited for Rusty to bring their bags into the bedroom. There were two bedrooms in the suite, but he knew they would only be using the one bed.

When Rusty came back, he took his suitcase from Rusty's hand, leaned in to kiss him on the mouth, and then headed for the bed to open his bag.

"What was that for?" Rusty asked.

"Because I love you."

Rusty grinned. "I love you too."

"We'll figure something out, Rusty. Don't worry."

"I know we will. It'll be okay."

God, I hope so.

Two hours later, found them surrounded by other riders as they all waited in the press room for the meet and greet to start. Lucas watched Levi and Curt as they stood in the corner talking. If he didn't know better, he would never have guessed they were lovers and building a life together. They didn't touch overly much, they didn't kiss in public, and they didn't really seem excessively affectionate with each other. Curt did lean in to tell something to Levi by getting close to his ear. It wasn't overtly obvious to anyone else, he noticed, but Curt did seem to linger a bit longer than someone who wasn't familiar with the other person. If he wasn't mistaken, Curt brushed a kiss across Levi's ear before he stood back.

The circuit's commissioner had been milling about the room for the last hour, talking to the riders and working the crowd. Now he stood at the front of the room and addressed everyone in general as he tried to get the riders into position. "All right, gentleman. We are about to let the press in. There is a table at the front of the room for you all to sit at while they ask questions and for you to sign autographs for the fans who will be allowed in after the press does their thing. If you are asked a question you are not comfortable with, please be cordial. You know how these press people are. They like to dig into personal lives."

Lucas nodded to Rusty indicating they should take a seat. Rusty tipped his chin in response before he moved toward the front of the room. Each rider's name was on a tented sign on the table. Lucas noticed Rusty's name was front and center next to Levi and his own was off to the left on the end. He wasn't surprised at the seating arrangement since Levi was the reigning World Champion and Rusty was to be the comeback kid of the year.

After all the riders had taken their places, the organizers opened the doors and the press came through them in a wave rushing to get near the front. The noise was deafening as the reporters started shouting questions out, trying to get the upper hand on the guy next to them.

They had one of the organizers standing in the front to keep the chaos at bay. "Miss Perez, your question?"

"Rusty. How are feeling? Are you ready to take the title this year from Levi?"

"You bet. I've never felt better, although Levi will be a tough contender for a repeat world championship, I'm sure."

"You got that right, Rusty," Levi said, slapping him on the shoulder. "I have big plans to repeat my run for the title."

"Mr. Johnson, your question?"

"Rusty, you went out with a pretty bad break last year. Are you completely healed?"

"Yes, sir. The doctors have released me from care, and I've had a chance to get on some great bulls during our off time."

"Mr. Marting, your question?"

"Levi, what's it like to be a gay bull rider in a very macho, testosterone filled environment? Do you get alone time with Curt so you two can have time for yourselves?"

Levi's face flushed red as he stood up behind the table. "My personal life is none of anyone's business. I don't promote the fact that I'm gay and in a relationship with another bull rider. We don't flaunt ourselves around the other riders, so I would appreciate it if you kept those types of questions out of this." He sat back down.

"Curt?" The guy wouldn't let it go.

"I agree with Levi. It's none of anyone's business what we do on our off time, so that question is moot. Let's move on, shall we?"

Lucas was amazed at how cool and collected the two of them were and how they handled the personal question from someone who had no business knowing anything about what they did on their off time. He definitely wanted to sit down and really talk one on one with these two guys. They were very open and out about their lifestyle and how it shouldn't make a damn bit of difference to anyone who they slept with.

With his hands now relaxed on the table, Lucas listened to the rest of the questions batted about the room, confident he and Rusty might actually be able to work this out and have the happiness he wanted with everything in his soul.

Chapter Twelve

The arena lights were turned down so only the spotlights were on. The riders circled the riding area, waiting for the music to start. Each one of them would be introduced as they walked up the wood plank to stand at the center of the shark tank with the spotlight on them for a brief moment. It was their moment of glory.

When it was his turn, Rusty walked up the plank, stood in the center and tipped his hat. The crowd went wild with cheers, whistling, and clapping. He smiled. It was good to be back.

As he walked down the other side, he took his place back around the outside area of the arena and waited for Levi to have his moment in the sun. They'd saved his introduction second to last and then introduced Levi as the reigning World Champion.

The lights went down again as they all headed back behind the chutes to get ready to ride.

Rusty went into the rider's room to grab his rope and rosin. Lucas was already there grabbing his stuff. "Hey."

"Hi."

"You ready for this?"

"I've been ready for this for months. It's hard not riding during the breaks. I get itchy."

"I know what you mean. Try having a broken leg and being out for months."

"Sorry, Rusty. I know that was tough on you, but I can't wait to see how you do tonight. Is your leg bothering you at all?"

"Nope. Feels good. I'll be stretching off and on while we are waiting for the others to ride."

"Will you be my rope man?"

"Of course. You don't have to ask."

"Well, I figured it was the nice thing to do." Lucas grinned as he slapped Rusty on the shoulder and then leaned in closer. "I don't want to assume anything just because you let me bury my cock in your ass earlier."

"Don't say that too loud. Mr. Coleman might be around." Rusty glanced over his shoulder. "Speak of the devil."

"Hey, Rusty. Lucas. You ready to ride?" Mr. Coleman asked, stopping at Rusty's side.

"Yes, sir."

Mr. Coleman touched the patch on Rusty's vest. "That insignia looks good on you."

"Thanks. I'll do my best to make you proud."

"I hope so." Mr. Coleman lowered his voice and moved closer. "Listen, Rusty. I hope you don't mind, but I need you to take Jessica out after the riding tonight. You know, to a bar or something. Be seen together." He slapped Rusty on the back, grinned and then turned on his heel to head for the door. "Ride well, boys!"

"Well fuck."

"Somehow, I think this whole sponsorship with Coleman is going to bite us both in the ass, and I don't think it will be a pleasant experience."

Lucas nodded solemnly as they both slowly walked out toward the arena to get ready for round one.

All Rusty wanted to do was ride bulls. When did the whole thing get so damned complicated?

When it came Rusty's turn to ride, he grabbed his rope and climbed up the platform behind chute number three. He handed his rope to Lucas who helped the spotters wrap it around the bull's underside as he climbed over the fence to straddle the hefty animal.

This particular bull was one that tended to spin to the right, which would be right into Rusty's riding hand. His pick would be one to get him a good score if he could stay on for eight. The bull weighed about seventeen hundred pounds with a large set of horns that banged against the metal chute in his temperamental way of letting everyone know he was not happy to be there. Mischief Maker was his name and he'd lived up to it so far from what Rusty knew of his run last year. The bull's buck-off rate was up there with the best.

Rusty settled down on the back of the bull, thighs spread, spurs down, body straight, and exhaled slowly. He knew the drill. This wasn't his first rodeo, but the rush going on in his head almost made him high.

By the time they got the bull rope situated around the bull and Rusty did his wrap, he was ready. It all came down to this ride for him. Would he be able to stay on? Could he get a good score, enough to place high in the rankings?

Rusty glanced over and caught Lucas's gaze on him. His love. His friend. His everything.

Lucas grinned and mouthed *you got this.*

Trepidation cramped his belly. It was time, his turn for the guts and glory.

With a nod of his head, the gate banged open and his world spun on its axis. The bull did exactly what Rusty thought he would do. He spun into Rusty's riding hand, making it that much easier to stay on, but he wasn't prepared when the bull dipped low, spun to the left, and twisted his body almost completely around.

His grip on the rope tightened to almost painful, his legs screamed, his head snapped back, and he felt himself slipped to the side. *Shit!*

He hit the dirt with a sickening thud. He couldn't move. It hurt to breathe.

Stunned silence thickened around him.

He lifted his head, shook it, and then crawled several feet across the dirt in an effort to avoid the bull.

When breathing became easier, he pushed himself to his feet. The crowd exploded in a roaring chorus.

Rusty glanced up at the score board, sure he hadn't made eight.

Eight nine point zero.

He sighed heavily as he glanced back to the board to make sure he hadn't imagined it. *Nope.* When the announcers flashed the leader board up, his name now resided in the number two spot.

Shaking his head to clear the ringing in his ears, he walked toward the rider's gate.

Doc Milburn met him as he made it through and headed back toward the locker room. "You okay, Rusty?"

"Yeah. He rang my bell a bit, is all."

"How's the leg?"

"Feels fine although I think I tightened up too much. It's kind of achy at the moment."

"If you want me to look at it, I will."

"Nah. I think it's good. I need some more bull time, is all. A few more rides and I'll be good as new."

Rusty didn't think the doctor believed him, but he responded, "Okay."

Levi met him at the end of the row of metal chutes holding the bulls yet to be ridden. "You looked great, Rusty."

"Thanks, man." He rotated his shoulder and did a few squats. "I'm still a bit stiff and I thought for sure I hadn't made eight on that ride."

"You did, barely, but you did." Levi clapped him on the back.

Rusty glanced around him to make sure no one was close enough to hear. "Levi, can I talk to you alone for a few minutes? We can do it after everything is over or whatever. I don't want to throw off your concentration."

"Sure, Rusty."

"Thanks." Rusty nodded and walked down the tunnel toward the locker room to store his stuff for now. Tunnel wasn't a true description since it really only consisted of a few feet of rock wall, but sound echoed around the area like when you talked in a cave. The only place in the seating that could see down into this area was the sponsor's seating and even those were very limited. You had to be sitting in the exact right place.

It would be a bit before he had to ride again so he figured he would take a piss, put up his rope, and stretch out his muscles to keep them warmed up, plus he needed to be there for Lucas.

C.B. Parker met him at the entrance of the locker room, hands on his hips and a glare in his eyes. "Rusty."

"Yeah?"

"Nice ride."

"Thanks." Rusty tried to step around him, but the other man blocked his entrance. "Something I can help you with?"

"Well, maybe. I've heard a rumor."

"Rumor?"

"Yeah. Are you and Lucas lovers?"

"That's none of your business."

"You just answered my question then."

"Listen, man. Lucas and I are friends. We've been friends for a long time. Hell, we grew up in the same town, did junior rodeo, and all kinds of stuff together growing up."

"I don't mean to pry, Rusty, but you know how guys are on the circuit."

"I know. You all are constantly boasting about your conquests with each week we ride. I'm not that kind of guy. Who I have sex with isn't up for discussion."

"I'm okay with it either way, Rusty. Although I'm not gay myself, I don't care if there are guys on the circuit who are." C.B. laid his hand on Rusty's shoulder for a moment. "Be careful though. There are those who would love to ruin you." He dropped his hand and did the chin tip thing. "I see you got a new sponsor?"

"Yeah. Coleman Enterprises approached me during break."

"They are a good sponsor."

"Yes they are, but there are conditions to my sponsorship with them that I don't like."

"Some of these sponsors are a little too big for their britches, if you know what I mean. I've got one like that. I can't take a shit without them knowing about it."

Rusty nodded in agreement. Since the sponsorship had come through, he had been to more press conferences, parties, events, and in front of the camera than he'd done since he started riding. That was saying something since the riders did meet and greets as well as appearances all over the country when they stopped to ride.

A quick glance toward the sponsor's seating area revealed Mr. Coleman and Jessica sitting side-by-side near the front row. They each appeared to have some kind of drink in hand as they talked back and forth. Mr. Coleman looked his way, but he knew he couldn't really see him from where he stood behind all the metal chutes and gates.

He would have to be very careful how he acted and what he did. The whole thing sucked donkey balls.

"Hey. See you later. I need to get ready to ride."

"Thanks, C.B. I appreciate the support."

"No problem, man." C.B. tipped his hat before making his way around Rusty and heading down the tunnel area toward the chutes.

While Rusty made his way toward where his bag sat on the floor in the corner, his thoughts went back to his ride and his future. It hadn't been pretty, but he'd gotten the job done. He needed to figure out how to ride a lot better though, if he planned to make the championship event in October.

The locker room was empty at this time of the evening. Everyone was getting ready to ride. He'd been the first one up in the initial round and Lucas wasn't riding for a bit, so now he had time on his hands.

He reached into his gear bag to grab a bottle of water. Something crinkled beneath his hand as he felt around inside. Curious, he pulled it out only to find an envelope with his name scrawled across the front. *What the hell?* He turned is over before sliding his first finger under the flap to open it. The writing hadn't looked familiar, so he really wondered who it was from since he hadn't left his gear bag alone except for a little bit here and there.

Rusty,

I didn't want to call you with this news because I knew you would be getting

ready for the season to start.

I have left your father and I will be filing for divorce in the next couple of

months. This will be hard on your younger brothers, I know, but after he came

home that morning when you told him you were gay and I saw what he'd

done to you physically, I couldn't stay with him any longer. He is not the man

I fell in love with so many years ago if he could do that to his own son.

The home place will be fine. Your father can have it. I've got a small place in

town for now and I'll leave it up to your brothers if they want to live with me or

him. He really does need the help on the home place.

I don't want this to ruin your day, so just know that I love you and I'll be by your
                         side in spirit.
                         I love you and tell Lucas hi for me. I think you two are cute together.

                         Love, Mom.

Wow. He couldn't believe his mother left his father over his declaration. He knew she didn't agree with his father on his stand with the whole thing, but he didn't want to break up their marriage over his own sexuality.

Rusty refolded the letter and put it back in the envelope before stuffing it back down in his gear bag. This was a complete shock to his system. He never thought his parents would separate or divorce. They'd always been his rock, his own example of a loving relationship. The illusion was now broken into splintering pieces and it made him reevaluate his own thinking.

"Hey, Rusty?"

"Yeah?"

"Are you coming out to help Lucas? He's up in two rides."

"Yes. I'll be right there." He kicked his bag back into the corner, grabbed his water bottle, and rose to his feet. His world had just been turned on its axis and he had a lot of things to go over in his mind now. He would have to do some research on gay relationships in their home state before he said anything to Lucas. After all, he wanted to get married, have children, and be a family for the rest of his life. Now he wasn't so sure that would be able to happen and what if for some reason they broke up? Then what? "Damn it. I really don't have time for this right now."

He shoved his fingers through his hair and readjusted his hat on his head before heading out of the locker room. He could get really hurt if he didn't keep his mind on the game at hand. The last thing he needed was another injury.

When he got to the chutes, he glanced left to see which one Lucas was riding out of and then walked that way. Several of the other riders were working rosin into their ropes to help their glove hand stick and others were stretching their muscles to warm up. Everyone stopped for a moment to say hi to him as he walked by. Riders on the circuit were a close bunch of guys most of the time, helping each other out and giving each other encouragement on their rides. It was something he really enjoyed about his fellow riders.

Rusty climbed up on the back platform attached to the chute where Lucas was getting ready to climb onboard.

"I thought I'd lost you."

"No, I went to the locker room for a minute."

"You going to be my vest man?"

"Sure."

Lucas eased himself down on the back of the bull as one of the guys tightened his rope before he threaded it through his glove in the standard wrap bull riders used. There were a few who chose to do a little different wrap, one they called a suicide wrap, but only a few had the guts or the stupidity to use that one most of the time.

Rusty stood at Lucas's shoulder, his hand on his safety vest, ready to pull him out if the bull got too rambunctious. The bull did a little hop, banging his horns on the metal railing. The echoing clang reverberated through the soles of Rusty's boots.

The bull was a good pick for Lucas, Rusty knew, because it had a reputation for being very active on the ride, but also bucking and twisting to the outside of the rider's hand. As long as Lucas stayed focused and balanced, he should have a good ride.

A moment later, the bull hopped and stood straight up on his hind legs, almost knocking Lucas over backward in the chute. Rusty grabbed the back of his vest and hauled him up and out of the way.

"Thanks."

"No problem," Rusty replied, trying to bring his racing heart under control.

Riders knew the risks, each and every one of them, but they also did their best to limit those risks.

Rusty knew if he hadn't pulled Lucas to safety right then, his whole world would have been changed in an instant. Lucas could have been crushed under the weight of the massive bull, his body twisted into some grotesque shape no one would recognize. His back might have been snapped, leaving him totally paralyzed for the rest of his life.

Yes, things like this could happen daily, but it didn't make it any easier to accept when it was someone you loved.

Lucas glanced up, locking his gaze with Rusty's for a moment. Lucas grinned as he winked and then turned back to the task at hand. He nodded a moment before the gate flew open and the ride was on.

The bull twisted left, then right, kicking his hind feet out in an almost vertical buck that sent Lucas catapulting off the back of the animal and into the dirt. His time, two point seven seconds.

The crowd groaned as Lucas walked toward the rider's chute. One of the bull fighters grabbed his rope from the ground and handed it him with a slap on the back. He would get one more chance to make eight or he would be out of the final round.

Rusty jumped down from his position, so he could meet Lucas at the rider's gate.

"Fuck!" Lucas threw his bull rope to the ground. "Son of a bitch!"

"Easy."

"No, not easy, Rusty. That was the shittiest ride I've ever done. That bull was rank. I should have been able to cover him no problem."

"What happened then?"

"He twisted left, my body went right. I lost my balance and instead of correcting myself, I ended up off his side and in the dirt." Lucas pulled off his riding glove and threw it in the rapidly growing pile of stuff.

"You'll get the next one."

"I should have had that one! I should have had a ninety point ride, but I fucked it up and now I'm at the bottom of the rung, hoping to make it to the finals this week."

Rusty realized it was probably better to keep his mouth shut and let Lucas vent, but he couldn't keep quiet. He wanted to help his friend. "Grab your stuff and come with me."

Lucas looked doubtful, but he followed Rusty with his gear in hand.

After they dumped his stuff in the locker room next to Rusty's, the two of them headed out of the tunnel and down the other areas leading to the unused portion of the arena. Rusty wasn't thinking clearly at the moment. All he knew was he needed to help his lover get his head back on straight so he could ride in the next round.

When they reached the door to a lone set of bathrooms almost halfway around the other side of the arena from the riders, Rusty pushed Lucas through the door, slammed him against the wall and kissed him with all the passion and desire he was harboring in his body.

Lucas finally took control and pushed Rusty back.

Rusty dropped to his knees in front of Lucas, stripped his chaps off, flipped open his belt buckle and started working on the button at his waist.

"What the hell are you doing? We could get caught." Lucas's cock responded, coming to a full rock hard erection within moments.

"No one uses these bathrooms, Lucas. The riders are on the other side of the arena. No one knows we're here, and I figure a good orgasm will help you focus." Rusty took the head of Lucas's cock between his lips and sucked hard. He could feel Lucas getting harder by the second as he worked his cock with his mouth. Sucking Lucas off right here where they could get caught at any moment gave him a little thrill. He was beginning to think he might be into some of the kinkier things to do with sex, the more he got to experiment on his lover.

"Fuck yeah." Lucas moaned as he put his full weight on the wall behind him and then buried his hands in Rusty's hair, knocking off his hat.

The bobbing of his head to the rhythm he'd established would probably bring Lucas to climax quickly. Rusty fingered Lucas's balls, rolling the little nuggets in his hands as he continued to run his tongue around the head of Lucas's cock. After a moment, he let the cock go before he ran his tongue up and down the length of hard flesh.

Lucas's breath came out in rapid pants as his hips moved slightly in a jerking movement. Rusty could tell he was close even after that short period.

When he wet one finger with saliva and then shove it into Lucas's ass, his lover shot his load down his throat in a matter of seconds as he called out Rusty's name.

Rusty licked the sticky substance off his lover's cock in slow, languishing movements until Lucas's cock softened.

"Interesting show, gentleman. I will give you this, I've never seen anything so sexy in my life. May I join you?"

Chapter Thirteen

Lucas opened his eyes as Rusty spun around. Standing in the doorway to the bathroom was Jessica Coleman.

Son of a bitch.

"Jessica." Rusty climbed to his feet. "I can explain."

Jessica held up her hand as she walked toward them. "No need, Rusty. I knew you were gay the moment I met you a few years ago. I thought it was kind of funny that my father insists on us being seen together when you have no interest in me whatsoever."

Lucas pulled his boxers and pants back up, fastening them at the waist before he buckled his belt. He wasn't sure what to do. Coleman wasn't his sponsor, but they sure were Rusty's and if Jessica felt like blowing their cover, Rusty would be out a lucrative sponsorship deal.

When Jessica got to their side, she reached out and started unbuttoning Rusty's shirt. "I've never seen two guys have sex before. It was really hot."

"Jessica."

She glanced up at Rusty as a sadistic grin spread across her face. "Yes?"

"We can't do this."

"Do what, Rusty? I'm not doing anything other than opening your shirt. I do like your chest, and the bit of hair that runs from your nipples to what waits behind your fly is really sexy." She ran a fingernail down Rusty's chest until she reached the waistband of his pants.

Lucas stood frozen to the spot where Rusty had just sucked him off, unable to react to what she was suggesting.

"What do you want to keep this quiet?" Rusty asked, pushing her hand away from the front of his pants.

"I want to watch Lucas fuck you in the ass and then I want you to fuck me."

A gasp escaped Lucas's mouth. Had she really just propositioned them so that she would keep quiet? Lucas shook his head. It sounded like something she would do.

"No, Rusty," Lucas said, finally voicing his concern over her blackmailing Rusty. "You know this won't be the one and only time this happens with her. She'll blackmail you over and over, dragging us both through hell at the same time. She's got both of us by the balls right now, but I say let her talk. If Coleman pulls his sponsorship, then so be it. We've talked about this."

Rusty never took his eyes off Jessica. "I know, Lucas. Don't worry. I'm not going to give in to her demands."

"You aren't?"

"No, because what I do on my off time is my own business and your old man can take that little piece of information and shove it up his ass. I don't care if you tell him about me and Lucas. We love each other and that's more important than any sponsorship you or your daddy can come up with."

"We'll see about that!" She stormed out of the bathroom, letting the door bang shut behind her.

"You sure about this, Rusty?"

"Yes. I should never have accepted his conditions in the first place. He's not going to run my life for me and I'm not some dancing puppet waiting for his approval. We'll be okay without his money."

"I love you."

"I love you too, Lucas. You mean more to me than any sponsorship ever could." Rusty reached for him, drawing him into a hug for a moment, before he leaned back and kissed him roughly. "Now, let's go get ready for the next round."

"Thanks for the blow job."

Rusty grinned. "You're welcome."

As they walked back down the deserted tunnel toward the bucking chutes, doubts surfaced in Lucas's mind. How would they function without the Coleman sponsorship? Did Rusty really think this through before he threw away his sugar daddy? He wasn't so sure.

When they got back to the riding area, Lucas wasn't surprised to see Mr. Coleman standing at the end of the metal gates watching for them. "Rusty, I need to talk to you."

"Yes, sir, but I can't right at the moment. The second round is about to start and I ride first." Rusty kept walking with Lucas right on his heels. He never looked back and Lucas was impressed and proud of his lover. Lucas glanced back over his shoulder. Mr. Coleman stood in the same spot with his mouth hanging open. After a second or two, he snapped it shut, turned on his heel, and disappeared back up the steps to the sponsor's area.

"Are you sure that was such a good idea?"

Rusty stopped and turned toward Lucas. "At this point it doesn't matter, Lucas. If he's going to pull, he's going to pull. No matter what I say to him, it won't make any difference at all." Rusty touched his arm. "Let's get our stuff out of the locker room and get ready to ride."

"Sure. Sounds good."

They grabbed their bull ropes, rosin, and a couple more bottles of water before they went out toward the chutes. The second long round would be starting soon and Lucas needed to qualify or this would be a short, disappointing weekend for him. He was thrilled Rusty had covered his bull, but it made him feel even more of an amateur than he already did around Rusty.

Rusty sat in a good position on the leader board, whereas Lucas didn't qualify on that round so he *had* to this round to be in the championship round.

When they reached the chutes, Lucas stopped Rusty with a hand on his arm. "Why did you tell Mr. Coleman you rode first? You ride second to last since you are number two on the leader board."

"I know, but I really wasn't ready to get into it with him right then. As far as I'm concerned, he can wait until after the event is over before he rips me a new asshole."

Lucas shook his head. Rusty had balls, that's for sure, if he was going to go nose to nose with the biggest sponsor on the circuit. Either way you sliced it, he was going to come out on the losing end. Lucas would be there when the chips fell. It was the least he could do for the man he'd fallen in love with.

The two of them stood on the upper deck of the platform watching as each rider took their turn in this long round. Someone could still knock Rusty down the ladder if they got a better score than he did, but Lucas didn't think that would happen. Rusty had done well and it was now up to the others to see what they could do.

A few of the riders who hadn't covered their bull in the first round, did on the second long round so the standings had shifted a bit. Rusty now sat in fourth place, but he had yet to ride in this round.

It came Lucas's turn to try to qualify.

After he eased himself down on the bull's back, he wrapped his hand, pounded on his closed fingers to try to tighten his hold a little more, flipped his chaps back out of his way, and gave a quick, jerky nod for them to open the gate.

Dust swirled as the bull charged out of the gate, twisted to the left as he kicked his hind legs out and up, and then went straight up in a bone jarring leap. Again, to the left, twisting his body first left, then right, the bull was bound and determine to dislodge the nuisance on his back. Lucas was just as determined to stay put. The eternity of eight seconds disappeared with the buzzer sounding. Lucas grabbed his rope to release his hand and jump free. The rope hung up.

The lights of the arena spun around in his vision as the bull continued to buck, slinging him around like a rag doll until the bull fighters got him loose.

With his face close to the dirt beneath him, he sat on his hands and knees for what seemed like hours.

"You okay, Lucas?" Marcus asked as he touched Lucas's shoulder. "Can you get up?"

"Yeah. Give me a second." Lucas knew Marcus from the years on the circuit. He was one of the best bull fighters around and if he wanted anyone watching his back it was Marcus.

Lucas climbed to his feet and walked toward the gates on shaky legs. He managed to glance up at the score board and was surprised to see a decent score. Eight five. He'd take it for now. His arm burned from being wrenched around, but he didn't think it was dislocated or anything. He could still move his fingers, bend his elbow, and lift his arm.

Rusty rushed to his side. "Lucas, are you okay?"

"Yeah. Just got the wind knocked out of me and wrenched my arm some."

"You should have Doc Milburn look at you."

"I'm fine, I said."

"All right then. I'm concerned is all. You'd feel the same way if it was me."

Lucas sighed as he looked at Rusty. He knew he would have felt the same way should it have been Rusty who was being tossed around like he didn't weigh anything at all. He'd actually been in that position a little when Rusty had the bull step on him last year. Not that Lucas would have confessed his love at that point, but he was still concerned about his friend's injury. "I know. I'm sorry. I'm okay, just sore."

"That's better. Don't shut me out, all right?"

"Sorry."

"You should ice it anyway, if nothing else. You qualified for the finals, so you're done for the night."

"Good. At least that's something."

"Yep. You rest."

"You need me to spot you, don't you?"

"I do, but I can get someone else. You rest that shoulder."

Lucas leaned closer to avoid anyone hearing him. "I love you."

"I know." Rusty grinned as he walked away.

Rusty wouldn't be riding for a few minutes, so Lucas had time to go to the doc's setup and get some ice.

When he headed around the back of the chutes and through the doorway toward the medical setup, he was stopped by Jessica.

"I want to talk to you, Lucas."

"I'm kinda busy right now. I need some ice for my shoulder."

"This will only take a minute."

"Okay. What is it?"

"You and Rusty seem to be quite cozy if you know what I mean."

"Yeah, so?"

"You convince him to do a three way, you, me, and Rusty and I will convince my father not to drop his sponsorship."

"You aren't fucking serious, are you?" The look she gave him told him she was completely serious. "Are you just turned on by two men having sex or what? I mean you do realize Rusty and I don't like women, right?"

She reached down and grasped his cock in her palm before she squeezed enough that it really hurt. "I'm sure you two can get it up for each other and then fuck me before you finish each other off. I like the thought of watching you two fuck like bunnies anyway."

"What the hell is wrong with you?"

Lucas glanced over her shoulder and caught the gaze of her father as he walked up close enough behind her to hear everything she said.

When he glanced back, her face had lost some of the smugness she'd been carrying when she walked up to him, realizing she wasn't getting a reaction from him. "I like new adventures in my sex life. Why do you think I've fucked half the bull riders on the circuit? I like a challenge. I like sex. Watching you two earlier was the hottest thing I've seen in a long time and I haven't been double penetrated in a while. I'm ripe for it. I'm horny as hell, and I want you two."

"Jessica Ann Coleman!"

She spun around so fast, she almost lost her balance. "Dad?"

"What's wrong with you, young lady? I don't believe what I heard come out of your mouth."

"Daddy, it's not the way it sounded. I found Rusty and Lucas down in one of the bathrooms having sex. Well, Rusty was giving Lucas a blow job." She stepped closer to her father. "Daddy, they're gay. They are lovers. You don't want that kind of thing tied with Coleman Enterprises, do you? I think you should cancel Rusty's sponsorship right now. If the press finds out he's gay and has another bull rider as his lover, it could ruin our reputation."

Lucas waited for Mr. Coleman to react to what Jessica had said. Rusty should be here for this, but he was getting ready for his ride. "Mr. Coleman, I can explain."

"All right, Lucas, go right ahead."

"Yes, Rusty and I are gay. We are lovers or have been for a few months. We love each other, Mr. Coleman, and there is nothing wrong with that. If you don't want Coleman Enterprises associated with a gay bull rider, then so be it. Rusty and I have discussed it and we are both okay with you pulling your sponsorship if that's what you want to do, but you have to understand one thing. What goes on in our bedroom is our business, no one else's. We don't flaunt ourselves out in public, kissing, caressing or doing any of those things. If you choose to keep sponsoring Rusty, then you can rest assured neither of us will do anything to put a black mark on the Coleman name. With that being said, we won't be blackmailed or forced to hide our love if we are asked about it either." Lucas stepped closer. "If you're afraid of negative publicity, you might want to look a little closer to home and clean up some of the stuff being said about your daughter. I'm sure you heard her since you were standing very close. All you have to do is talk to some of the riders and you'll get the full story if you want to have it." Lucas turned around to head down the walkway toward medical, but before he did he turned back to Mr. Coleman and said, "Rusty is headed for the World Championship this year and I really think he's going to win. You would do well to have him represent you."

Lucas tipped his hat, turned back toward the medical tent and kept moving. His shoulder throbbed, his head hurt, and his heart was in turmoil. He hoped to God that Rusty wouldn't hate him for what he'd done. It needed to be said and if it meant they lost the sponsorship, then it was meant to be.

He reached the medical tent, and walked inside. "Need some ice for that shoulder, Lucas?"

"Yeah, Doc. Thanks. It hurts pretty bad right now."

"I'm sure it does. You're lucky you didn't dislocate it." Doc Milburn pushed around on the socket, raised his arm a couple of times, before putting it back down by Lucas's side. "You sprained it probably, but ice and meds will fix you up."

"I appreciate it."

As soon as Lucas was taped up with an ice bag on his shoulder, he went back out behind the chutes. If he was lucky, he hadn't missed Rusty's ride.

"Now up, the circuit's comeback kid, Rusty Arnold. Rusty covered his bull in round one with a very nice score. With only a few of the riders covering both bulls in these long rounds, Rusty has a chance to take the lead and really make this a great weekend."

Lucas hauled himself up on the platform behind the chutes so he could see Rusty and watch the ride from a great vantage point.

Rusty had gotten himself settled on the back of the bull and was wrapping his hand before he gave the nod. Lucas could see him scoot forward to center himself on the animal.

The nod came, the gate exploded open, and the bull went wild. Rusty's hand whipped back and forth, steadying him in his position as the heavy animal bucked and kicked, trying desperately to dislodge the man on his back. Rusty held on. The buzzer sounded indicating eight seconds was over.

Rusty released his hand and jumped clear. When he glanced up at his score, he pumped his fists in the air at the eight seven point five score. With that ride, he was now in first place for the event and in a good position to take home the prize for the weekend.

Lucas worked his way down to the gate to wait for Rusty. He needed to tell him what had transpired with Mr. Coleman before someone else got the word to him.

As Rusty came around the corner and Lucas got close to him, Mr. Coleman stepped out of the shadows in front of Rusty.

"Let's talk, Rusty." Mr. Coleman turned on his heels expecting Rusty to follow.

Rusty hadn't seen him before he started after Mr. Coleman.

Lucas didn't know whether to follow or not, but he figured he was already in this up to his ass. The least he could do was be there in support of the most important man in his life. The moment Lucas rounded the corner, he could hear Mr. Coleman.

"Rusty, I know about you and Lucas Jacks."

"I assumed as much, Mr. Coleman."

"I also found out some things about my daughter today that I'm not very proud of."

Rusty didn't respond.

"Lucas, will you join us?" Mr. Coleman motioned for him to come forward as soon as he'd made it around the corner. "You're part of this, too."

"Lucas, what's going on?"

"Jessica approached me when I was headed back to get ice for my shoulder. She said some things that weren't very nice. Mr. Coleman heard her, but in the process he also found out about us."

"Mr. Coleman, I want you to—"

"Rusty, please, let me finish before you try to explain something I already understand. Lucas told me about how you two are gay and that you are lovers. I want you to know I'm okay with that. I have a son from another marriage who is also gay. He told me last Christmas. It was a bit of a shock to us as his family, but it is something I've come to realize doesn't define the man you are, it just means you are in love with someone who happens to be the same sex you are. It doesn't mean there is anything wrong with you. When I talked about negativity with this sponsorship, I was more concerned that you would be caught with a prostitute or something that would look bad. I had no idea this is what you were worried about."

"You don't have a problem with us being gay on the circuit?"

"No son, I don't. I would appreciate it though if you two weren't flaunting it around a lot, only because I know some of the other riders aren't comfortable with this kind of thing."

"You aren't pulling your sponsorship?"

"Nope. I hope we can have a nice long, healthy, profitable relationship, Rusty. I think you are going to be the rider to contend with this year, and I want Coleman Enterprises to be your major sponsor."

Rusty held out his hand. "Thank you, Mr. Coleman. I'm surprised but very pleased."

"I trust you two to make sure you are professional about things."

"Yes, sir. Of course."

"That's all I can expect." He tipped his hat as he walked around them. "See you at the next stop."

Rusty grinned as he stepped up to Lucas. "Wow. I hadn't expected that at all."

"Me either."

"We definitely have some things to celebrate tonight. You ready for a beer?" Rusty asked as they turned back toward the tunnel to the locker room.

"Hell, yes. I could use a couple of cold ones to wash this dirt and grit out of my mouth."

"Me too. Let's grab our stuff and head to that honky-tonk I saw."

"Are you sure you don't want to find a gay bar?"

"Nah. I'm okay with the beer joint. Besides, you won't be up to doing anything tonight anyway, cowboy."

"The hell you say!"

"We'll see later then, but I'm not taking bets on having sex tonight."

After they grabbed their stuff, they walked out to the back of the chutes. The arena was emptying now that the riding was over, but a few fans hung around for autographs afterwards. All the riders stuck around for that since it was a great way to meet the fans.

Rusty and Lucas walked out together, making their way down the line of people waiting for signatures. Lucas was stopped by a cute little blonde haired girl who was about twelve. "Hi there."

"Hi." She blushed a deep red. "Can you sign my book for me?"

"Certainly, sweetheart. Who do you want me to make this out to?"

"Angela."

"What a pretty name for a beautiful girl."

He wrote, *To Angela. May all your dreams come true. Love, Lucas Jacks.* When he handed it back to her, she clutched it to her chest and looked up with doe eyes. He couldn't help himself, he leaned in and kissed her on the cheek. "Be happy, little one. Find you a great guy."

After a brief smile in her direction, he turned and kept moving. He signed a few more autographs before they got to the end of the line and headed to the cabs waiting for people outside the arena, who needed a ride home after drinking too much. The shoulder he'd injured ached like a son of a bitch, and he was ready for that beer.

They climbed into the cab, slamming the doors behind them.

"I talked to Levi earlier and mentioned we or I wanted to talk to him."

"Oh?"

"Yeah. I want to find out how he's handling the relationship with Curt being out and open within the circuit."

"Sounds good."

"Do you want to be there?"

"Yeah. I'd like to hear how they are handling it too."

"Maybe after we have our beers, we can go somewhere quiet."

"All right."

They pulled up to the bar a few minutes later. The crowded parking lot told him that there would, more than likely, be a lot of people inside. He didn't mind though. The adrenaline rush of riding took some time to come down from and a big, noisy crowd helped.

As they walked inside, they were greeted by several fans and other riders. There were handshakes, back slaps, and general how are things going type greetings. Many of them hadn't had the chance to talk to Rusty about his return, so they spent the first hour talking to old friends over a beer. Lucas stayed in the background mostly, willing to give Rusty the limelight he deserved after his awesome rides today.

He noticed Levi and Curt sitting in a corner booth, heads together. He watched them as he sipped his beer. They were obviously not afraid to show their commitment to each other even in a bar like this. They touched, held hands, kissed a couple of times, and shared a drink. It was nice to see, and no one seemed to have a problem with them showing their affection for each other in a public manner. They didn't get raunchy or anything, just simply acted like two people in love.

Lucas noticed the gold band winking in the overhead lighting on Curt's finger. *Interesting.* He hadn't heard about any wedding between the two, but since they seemed to be wearing matching wedding bands, there must have been one during the off season.

It made him wonder if he and Rusty would ever marry in the eyes of God, the state, and whomever cared to come. He thought about it for a moment, and decided, yeah, he'd like it if they got married someday, maybe after the truth of their relationship quit being the gossip of the town. It would seal things even more permanently than the 'I love you' they had exchanged already.

Rusty walked over and leaned in close to his ear. "Ready to talk to Levi and Curt?"

"Are you sure you want to disturb them? They seem pretty content right now."

"True," he said, glancing over in their direction. "We can always wait until tomorrow before we have to go to the arena."

"Sounds good." Lucas put his empty beer bottle on the bar. "I'm beat."

"Do you want to head back?"

"Yeah."

"Let me pay our tab and we'll go." Rusty signaled for the bartender so he could tally up their drinks.

Lucas leaned heavily on the barstool while he waited for Rusty. His shoulder was killing him and he was downright exhausted from the day. Tonight might be a cuddle night only in bed, and he wondered if Rusty would mind. He thought it might be nice to curl up against Rusty, lay his head on his shoulder and fall asleep like that.

A moment later, he heard a ruckus start near the door. When he looked over the heads of the patrons between himself and the double doors, he hoped he wasn't seeing what he thought he might be. Jessica Coleman was making a scene at the door. "Great. Just fucking great."

"What?"

"Jessica Coleman just came in and she sounds like she's already drunk off her ass."

"Do you know who my father is? He's the biggest sponsor of the bull riders. His business is Coleman Enterprises and if you don't fucking let me in this building, he'll come down here and shut this place down."

"Oh wonderful," Rusty said in a whisper.

The bouncer stood near her. "Ma'am, you've already had too much to drink. Would you like me to call you a cab?"

"No! I fucking want one of these studs in here to take me back to his room and fuck me."

"Wow," Lucas added. "She's on a roll. If her daddy saw her now, he'd be having a shit fit."

"You aren't kidding."

She shook off the bouncer and headed right for them. Lucas and Rusty tried turning their backs so she wouldn't see them. Too late.

"You! Rusty Arnold."

Rusty turned toward her when she said his name. "Jessica, you need to go back to your room and sleep it off."

She laughed. The sound was hollow and lonely. When she pointed to Carl Whistler, she moved closer. "I bet a lot of you guys don't know what goes on behind closed doors, do you?"

"Oh, shit." Lucas wanted to grab her, clamp his hand over her mouth, and throw her outside.

"Yep. I'm talking about two of your trusted riders fucking on the side."

"What are you talking about?"

Carl got closer to her as she kept on talking. Lucas and Rusty knew he was a homophobic and would be difficult to shut up once he found out dirt on someone.

"Yep." She spun around. "Rusty Arnold and Lucas Jacks are fuck buddies. I saw Rusty giving Lucas a blow job at the arena. Got him off and everything."

Carl's eyes narrowed as he looked past her shoulder right into Lucas's gaze. "That so?"

"She's drunk, man. She doesn't know what she's talking about." This came from C.B. Parker who was standing next to Carl when shit started to go down.

"I did too. I saw them."

"Are you a fucking queer, Jacks?"

Lucas stepped forward. He'd had enough of this shit. What they did in the bedroom was their own business and no one else's, but shit was coming to a head and he needed to shut it down. "None of your God damn business, Carl."

"What the hell is this circuit coming to? Levi and Curt are all over each other in the corner over there and now you? I'm done with you fucking faggots." Carl pushed his way to the door and disappeared.

C.B. stepped forward. "We are here to unwind people. Grab a beer and have a good time. The excitement is over."

"No it's not! You guys don't care whether Lucas and Rusty are fucking each other when y'all aren't looking?"

"Jessica, you're one to talk. You've fucked half the circuit at one time or another." J.M. Moneymaker stood next to C.B. "Lucas is right. What they do in the privacy of their room is no one's business."

Lucas was shocked. To have the support of two of the biggest names on the pro circuit meant a lot. If those two didn't care, most of the others wouldn't either or would keep their mouths shut about it.

The crowd that had gathered disbursed back to what they were doing before everything started, leaving Jessica without the audience she'd come there for.

"Jessica, go on back to your room," Rusty said. "No one here wants to hear the shit you are slinging."

"You'll be sorry you didn't take me up on my offer, Rusty. Your days on this circuit are numbered." She spun on her heels and disappeared back through the few people who were still standing by, waiting for something to happen that would liven up their night.

Rusty exhaled on a rush as he turned back toward Lucas. "Let's get out of here."

"Wait a second. I want to thank a couple of people." Lucas stopped at C.B. and J.M.'s side. "Thank you for standing up for us."

"Not a problem, Lucas," J.M. replied. "It's no skin off my nose what you do when I'm not looking. Just don't come onto me, okay, buddy?" J.M. laughed as he slapped Lucas on the back. "I don't swing that way."

C.B. nodded too before going back to his beer and the pretty little brunette standing next to him.

Lucas went back to Rusty's side and then tipped his head to the left to indicate he was ready to leave. Rusty followed him outside so they could hail a cab.

Snow had begun to fall, blanketing the streets with a white sheen. Several footsteps were visible in the accumulation, letting them know this was a city that never slept. There were always people on the streets going or coming. It was something unique about New York that made the place fascinating to newcomers.

Cabs whizzed by. Lights flickered on and off. The snow crunched under their boots as they stopped near the curb to try to flag down a cab.

Lucas went to raise his arm, forgetting for a moment about his sore shoulder. "Shit, that hurt."

"Let me," Rusty said, standing on the curb with his hand in the air.

Several more cabs flew by so fast it was a wonder anyone near the street wasn't hit by the cars rushing by.

Finally, a cab slowed and stopped in front of them. The parking at the Gardens was difficult at best. That's why they'd taken a cab to the arena, and Lucas was glad they had.

After they slipped inside and Rusty gave the name of the hotel where they were staying, the door banged shut, and they were off at the speed of sound. They both gripped the seats trying desperately to stay upright as the cab went around the corners on what seemed to be two wheels. Lucas thought for sure he was about to die. The guy whipped between cars where surely there wasn't enough room to maneuver, but the guy did it without hitting anyone else.

Lucas didn't breathe until they'd pulled up in front of the hotel and the door was jerked open by the bellman standing at the curb.

"Welcome, gentleman," the bellman said as he waited for them to exit the car.

Rusty paid the driver as Lucas slid out and stood. His heart was racing and his palms were sweaty. He rode bulls for a living and yet driving in New York scared the hell out of him. He laughed nervously. "Some ride, eh?"

"Right now my balls are in my throat, buddy. I thought for sure we were going to die before we got here."

"Yeah, me too." Lucas gave a rueful laugh as they approached the door now being held by the bellman.

"Enjoy your evening, sirs."

"Thank you. We will," Lucas replied as they moved through the doorway into the lobby of the hotel. He hadn't noticed the ornate gold trim on everything until now. They say things are bigger in New York. He could believe it as he and Rusty made their way toward the elevator. Marble floors echoed their boot steps. People moved every which way, rushing around like they had somewhere important to go. Lucas decided right then and there, he would never live in the city. He was a country boy at heart and didn't want to live anywhere without open fields, cattle, horses, swaying grass, and silence. What he wouldn't give right now for a few minutes of silence.

As the doors to the elevator *wooshed* open, Lucas stood back so the throng of people could exit before he and Rusty got inside. When the doors closed, they were enveloped in a bit of quiet. *Thank God. I can't wait to get to our room and shut out the world with its negativity, homophobic people, and stress.*

Rusty took his hand before he leaned in and kissed him on the mouth.

"The world will disappear in a few minutes and we can relax."

"Thanks."

"You're welcome."

They reached their floor a few seconds later as the doors slid open. Lucas stepped out and walked down the hall to the left, with Rusty trailing behind him by a few feet. He wanted a drink, to put his feet up, and forget the craziness of the night. His shoulder throbbed, his head felt like it wanted to explode, and all he could think about beyond that was spending time with the man he'd fallen in love with. He didn't want to think of futures, what they would do now, or anything else for the time being. Life could stop for a few moments, and he would be content.

He slipped the keycard into the lock before he pushed open the door to their suite. He barely made it to the couch before he toed off his boots and sank onto the leather cushions with a sigh.

"Can I get you a beer?"

"Please."

Rusty returned a moment later with a beer for each of them as he sat down beside Lucas.

"How's the shoulder?"

"Sore. I should ice it some more before we go to bed."

"You probably should, yes."

Lucas leaned his head back on the couch and then turned his head to glance at Rusty. "Why do people even care that we love someone of the same sex?"

"I don't know, Lucas. It's baffled me for a long time. People are becoming more tolerant of it, but I think it will be a long time before they accept it."

"Are you sure you want to defy normal to be with me?"

"Of course I do. I love you."

Lucas sighed as he turned back and stared at the ceiling in their room. Everything seemed so difficult. Trying to get people to accept them for who they are rather than who they loved, seemed to be a daunting task. One he wasn't so sure he could do.

"Do you love me?" Rusty asked, touching Lucas's face.

"Yes."

"Then it doesn't matter what others think."

"But it does, Rusty."

"Why?"

"Because I don't want to have to hide who I am anymore or who I love. I want to be able to kiss you in public. I want to be able to hug you when I feel like it. Right now, those things make others feel uncomfortable."

"It's their problem, not ours."

"I'm not sure I'm strong enough to battle their prejudices for the rest of my life."

"What are you saying?"

"I think you need to find someone else to love, Rusty, someone who can stand beside you and thumb their noses at normalcy. The world hates gays."

Rusty moved to straddle Lucas's hips and got right in his face. "I don't fucking care what is normal. I love you, and I'm not letting you walk away from us because you're scared."

"But what happens later? What if we get married, live in your house, and raise a family? Our kids will be laughed at and ostracized because they have two dads."

"Then we will teach them to be tolerable of those who are different than they are. We will love them through thick and thin. We will be the family everyone wants to be. As long as we love each other, it doesn't matter what others think. Any children we have together will be blessed with parents who love them."

"I just don't know, Rusty."

Rusty moved off him and sat back on the couch. "You have to do what you have to do, Lucas. If your love for me isn't strong enough to withstand the problems that will arise over time, then I'm sorry. I love you with all my heart, but I can't love you for both of us. You have to decide what is important to you. If I'm important enough for you to turn your back on conventional thinking, then we can build a life together." After Rusty got to his feet, he leaned down, kissed Lucas on the mouth, and then walked toward the bedroom door. "Think about that for a while.

When you are ready to love me like I deserve to be loved, then find me."

Chapter Fourteen

Rusty closed the door to the bedroom in the hotel room. He knew he had to be tough for Lucas, but his heart ached, and his chest hurt from the pain he was feeling. He loved Lucas with everything he had, but Lucas had to figure out what he wanted to do.

A tear slipped down his cheek. At this point, he didn't know what else to do except give Lucas the means to break his heart if he walked away.

A sigh escaped his lips as he pushed off the door and moved toward the bathroom. A hot shower would feel really good right now. He shut the bathroom door, turned on the spraying shower, shucked his clothes, and then stepped inside. The water cascaded over him as he leaned against the tile wall and bent his head down. He tried washing away his sorrow.

He stood that way for several minutes before he raised his head, wiped his eyes, and began to wash away the dirt and grime from his ride today. He'd done well on his bulls. He couldn't complain about his scores. His position on the leader board was solid and he was on track to win this event. It would make his comeback all the more sweet if he took home the prize at the first event after his accident.

When the water began to cool, he shut it off, grabbed the towel from the hook near the shower, and dried himself off. With the towel around his hips, he moved into the bedroom to grab some clean shorts out of his duffle.

Once he had on his shorts, he pulled the covers back on the bed and slid beneath the cool white sheets. Tonight would be a lonely night, he was afraid, as he put his arm behind his head and stared at the ceiling. He wouldn't give in and go to Lucas.

He said his piece, and now it was up to Lucas to decide what he really wanted.

The night tiptoed by as Rusty tossed and turned in the big bed. He wondered where Lucas had slept since he never came to their bed during the night. Sunlight crept into the room in a slow slice of light that lengthened on the floor. Rusty hadn't slept much at all which would make riding difficult today for the final round. His mind would be elsewhere, he knew, but he'd get over it. If Lucas decided he didn't want to fight for them, Rusty would figure things out and move on. It wasn't as if he had a choice in the matter, really. He couldn't make Lucas love him or want to spend his life with him, if he didn't want to. *Damn stupid asshole!*

Rusty got up and slipped on his jeans. They didn't have to be at the arena until late this evening since the final round didn't start until eight. They were required to be there a couple of hours beforehand, to do the meet and greet with the fans, but other than that, he had the day to himself.

When he opened the door to the bedroom, he wasn't prepared for the dead silence of the room. Nothing moved. He glanced at the door across the room that led to the second bedroom. It was closed tight. *Lucas must have slept there.* Rusty shook his head before he walked into the kitchen area to start some coffee. There wasn't anything to eat, but they did stock the bar and the coffeemaker. He'd have to order breakfast, he guessed.

"Rusty?"

He spun around to find Lucas standing behind him. "Yeah?"

"I'm sorry."

"Sorry?"

"Yes." Lucas leaned in and kissed him on the mouth. "I'm scared, very scared at what might happen in the future. I guess I need to not worry so much about other people and what they think of you and me. It's their problem and they need to deal with it. People won't understand. I get that. It will be difficult for us, I know, but if we face it together, we will win in the end because we love each other."

"That's right. We love each other and together we can do anything."

Lucas pulled him into a hug, not a pacifying hug, but a real honest to goodness I love you hug. "Don't ever shut me out of our bedroom again."

"I didn't. The door wasn't locked."

"When you shut it between us, it was as if you shut me out of your life."

"No, you needed to understand that you had to deal with your fears on your own. I love you, but I can't fix everything for you. Even though we are partners in this, there are going to be times that you will have to make up your own mind about things. Now that you've realized we can make this work if we do it together, then you'll be able to love me how I deserve to be loved, like the partner in your life and not just a convenience."

"You were never just a convenience, Rusty, never."

"You made me feel that way last night when you were ready to throw everything we have together out the window because of your fear of the future."

"I'm sorry. I have to be strong in my belief that we are meant to be together. With you by my side, I can overcome the fear of the unknown. I know I can."

He kissed Lucas, a full blown tongue twisting kiss that made his cock stand up and ache for the soft warmth of his lover's ass. He needed the connection, the feeling of oneness that he'd always had with Lucas when they made love. "I love you."

"I love you too."

"Let me make love to you."

Lucas nodded as he took Rusty's hand and let him back into the bedroom. Neither of them said a word as they slowly undressed each other, touching and feeling bare skin as the clothes fell away. Rusty ran his tongue over Lucas's chest, stopping to nibble on his erect nipples as he worked his way down his abdomen. Lucas's cock stood erect against his belly with a small drop of pre-cum glistening on the tip. Rusty licked it away before taking the head of Lucas's cock into his mouth. Lucas hummed deep in his throat, the sound reverberated down Rusty's spine. He loved to make Lucas lose control.

He let his fingers outline Lucas's balls, kneading the soft sack with his hand. When he dipped his finger into Lucas's back hole, his lover shoved his hands into his hair and pulled his face closer to his groin.

"Fuck, Rusty. So good."

Rusty bobbed his head up and down, tonguing Lucas's length to bring him to the brink of climax before he stopped, encircled the cock and squeezed to forestall Lucas's impending orgasm. "Not yet."

"You'd better hurry then, because I'm about to blow."

Rusty lead Lucas to the bed, grabbed the lube from the nightstand and then pushed Lucas down so that his ass was in the air, his feet were spread, and he was open to the invasion to come. "Spread your cheeks, Lucas. I want to see that gorgeous hole waiting for me."

Lucas did as he was told, putting one hand on each cheek to open for his lover.

"Nice." Rusty dribbled lube down the crack of Lucas's ass, and he hissed in response. "I know it's cold, but it will warm up fast once I'm in."

"Hurry."

Rusty slicked up his cock with the lube before tossing the tube onto the bed. "I'm coming home." Rusty nudged the head of his cock at Lucas's asshole. The slow glide of skin against skin almost hurt, it felt so good. The soft warmth that surrounded him had his breaths coming out choppy. His heart raced. His body tingled from his scalp to his toes. It was the first time he'd gone bare with Lucas and the feeling was nothing he could have imagined.

"Oh, God, Rusty."

"Brace yourself. I'm going to fuck you hard and fast."

Rusty thrust his hips forward, burying his entire length in the welcoming envelop of Lucas's back channel. After a moment of deep breathing to keep from coming too fast, Rusty began to thrust in earnest. Lucas had reached down and was fucking himself with his hand as Rusty thrust harder. "That's it, Lucas. Work that cock."

"I'm going to come."

"Not yet."

Lucas looked back over his shoulder. "The hell you say."

"Not yet. Hold on as long as you can. It'll be better."

"Fuck." Lucas groaned as his hand milked his cock fast. "God, I'm gonna die."

"Almost there."

He fucked Lucas so hard, they were banging the bed against the wall, making it thump loudly in a steady bang, bang, bang. He hoped there wasn't anyone in the room next door, but right now he didn't give a shit. He had his lover under him and he was going to enjoy every minute he was buried in Lucas's ass.

"God, Rusty. Let me come, please."

He panted hard as he continued to thrust. Every minute he was buried there was another minute of euphoria, another minute of bliss, another minute of all was right in the world.

When his climax hit, he groaned Lucas's name and finally gave Lucas permission to find his own release.

Lucas moaned softly as cum shot across the bed before he slumped down on the coverlet unable to move.

Rusty removed his softened cock and walked into the bathroom on shaking legs. When he stopped to look in the mirror, what he saw made him smile. Contentment stared him back in the face.

When he walked back into the bedroom, Lucas hadn't moved from where he'd left him sated on the bed. A quick slap to his bare ass brought him upright on the bed. "Unless you plan to fuck me again right now, save that shit for later."

"Is that so?"

"Yep."

"We'll see." Rusty glanced at the clock. "I need some breakfast." He grabbed his clothes from the floor and slipped on his boxers and pants.

"Me too," Lucas replied, grabbing his own clothes. "I say we go downstairs and get something to eat."

"I'll text Levi and Curt. We can see if they will meet us down there."

"Sounds good."

After a couple of texts to Levi, Rusty pulled on his boots, adjusted his hat, and headed for the door with Lucas on his heels. He couldn't wait to talk to his friends about how they were handling being gay on the circuit. He hoped they could give him some insight to how to live within the bull riding community and still be happy in a relationship.

When the door to the elevator opened on the ground floor, Rusty took a right and headed for the café within the confines of the hotel. They hadn't stopped there before, but he'd seen it when they checked in. It was cozy and off to the back so they could have some privacy for their conversation.

Levi and Curt sat near the rear and waved them over when they stopped at the hostess.

"I see them back there. Thank you." Quick strides took them to the table. "Thanks for meeting with us, you two."

"Sure, Rusty." Levi nodded. "Have a seat and tell us what we can do to help."

The waitress brought over two more coffee cups and asked if they wanted coffee. "Yes, please," Lucas replied. "I need something strong with lots of caffeine. I didn't sleep well last night."

After they doctored their cups of fortification, Rusty took a deep breath and said, "How are you two handling being on the circuit?"

"What do you mean, Rusty?" Levi asked as he sat forward in the chair.

"Okay. Let me take a step back. Lucas and I are in a relationship, much the same as you and Curt. What I want to know is how are you handling trying to keep your personal lives separate from what everyone expects on the road?" Rusty folded his hands on the table and waited, afraid he wouldn't like what Levi had to say.

Levi glanced at his partner before his gaze settled back on Rusty. "I didn't realize you were gay, Rusty."

"Yeah. I haven't been very vocal about it, but yeah. I knew back in high school."

"Curt and I have been lucky. We haven't caught much flack over being gay on the circuit. I guess that might be because I was pretty open about my sexuality, if anyone took the time to ask. I wasn't pushy about it like going after guys I knew weren't into that sort of thing. I usually kept things private, if you know what I mean. When Curt and I started seeing each other, we weren't in your face with it. We spent our time together in the privacy of our room. There weren't any public displays of affection or anything like that. After Curt was hurt riding last year, I realized that I didn't care anymore if people weren't comfortable with us being together. I almost lost him and it made me think really hard about what I wanted."

Rusty contemplated what Levi said. His relationship with Lucas was much the same thing, private. He knew what he wanted and that was a life with Lucas no matter who approved or didn't approve. He knew his family wouldn't like it, or at least his father and Russell, but they would have to get over it. He had decided to live his life the way he wanted and to hell with whatever others thought. "I appreciate your honesty, Levi."

"You're welcome." He turned to Curt and said, "Is there anything you want to add?"

"Not really, except one thing. If you love each other, then nothing else matters. You see, I thought my parents didn't care about me, didn't care what I did, and didn't care who I loved. When Levi and I went to tell them about us, they were ecstatic about our relationship. It floored me. I never expected that at all. They were completely okay with me being gay and loving another man."

"My father lost his shit when he found out about me," Rusty said. "My twin brother, Russell, did too. My mom is okay with it as are my younger brothers. I don't know if my father or Russell will ever come around."

"They may or may not, but you can't live your life worrying about them. Your love for Lucas will see you through everything, if it's strong enough. There will be people who don't get it and there is nothing you can do to change their minds. It's their problem, not yours." Curt took Levi's hand in his, threading their fingers together.

"I appreciate you two taking the time to talk to us. Lucas has been having some trouble dealing with it being out in the open. We haven't talked to his family, but he's sure they won't be supportive either and will probably disown him." Rusty reached under the table and squeezed Lucas's hand to help reassure him he was the most important thing in his life.

"That's a chance you take loving someone of the same sex."

"I know." Rusty sighed before he picked up his coffee and took a healthy sip. He needed fortification for what he had in mind. For now, they needed to get through this weekend and ride like their balls were on fire.

When they headed to the arena later on that evening, Rusty had a lot on his mind. He needed to ride well in the final round to get the points. It was still very early in the season, but every point could make or break him when October rolled around again. He wanted to be on top and to be there, he had to win.

As they stowed their gear bags in the locker room, Rusty was lost in thought.

"You okay?" Lucas asked, touching his shoulder.

"Yeah. I'm just thinking, is all."

Lucas looked around for a moment before he leaned in and kissed Rusty on the mouth. Luckily, there wasn't anyone else in the locker room.

"You're taking a big chance doing that here."

"I know, but I needed to feel your lips under mine before I rode." Lucas touched his cheek. "I love you, you know."

"I love you too. Be careful out there tonight. I know your shoulder is probably still bothering you."

"A little, yes, but I'll be okay."

"Don't try to be Superman, Lucas."

"I won't. Besides, you're the golden boy. You need to win this."

"I'll do my best."

"If you cover your bull in the final round, you will win. You're sitting in first place right now." Lucas put his hand on Rusty's shoulder, giving it a little squeeze of encouragement. "Go get 'em, tiger."

Rusty smiled before they walked out together to find out which bull they'd drawn for the final round. He hoped it was one that was rank and would give him a good ride, but he also hoped it wasn't Lucifer's Chaos. That bull was the best on the circuit and one not too many guys had been able to ride.

When they found out the order in which they would ride, Lucas smiled. "I think you'll do well on Jack's Tornado."

"I hope so. I need a good ride to maintain the lead."

"You'll do fine." Lucas moved over to a spot behind the chutes where they could stretch. "Do you need me to help you stretch out?"

"You do that and I doubt I'll make a good ride because I'll be as hard as a rock trying to maintain my balance on the bull."

Lucas quirked an eyebrow as he shook his head. "Not me."

"Yes, you."

A grin spread across his face as he moved farther down the railing to tie his bull rope on so he could rosin it up. Lucas would ride before Rusty since Rusty was first on the leader board, which meant he'd go last.

When it was Lucas's turn, he hopped up on the platform behind the chute he was assigned, leaving Rusty to watch him from below. *Man, do I love this guy.* Rusty saw him hand his rope over to the guy who would get it around the bull as he threw his leg over the metal side and got ready to lower himself down.

The bull stood completely still during the entire get ready sequence, making Rusty nervous. He'd never seen a bull that still during the prep. They usually tossed their head, leaned against one side or the other, or they shifted back and forth. This bull did nothing. If he wasn't sure the damned thing was alive, he'd think the bull was sleeping as it stood there waiting for the nod of Lucas's head.

The moment Lucas nodded, all hell broke loose. The bull shot out of the gate kicking and leaping while Lucas's head was snapped back so hard, Rusty heard the pop of his neck. Lucas leaned too far forward on the buck just as the bull snapped his head up, nailing Lucas in the face. He went limp on the ride as the buzzer sounded. His body was tossed like a rag doll as the bull fighters worked to get his hand free. It appeared Lucas was unconscious when his body hit the dirt with a sickening thud.

Rusty couldn't move. His first instinct was to rush out there to help his lover, but he knew he couldn't.

Medical personnel moved out to his side.

Lucas didn't respond when the guys rolled him over.

The medical team signaled for a stretcher.

Rusty's heart was in his throat. *Lucas, wake up, please wake up.*

They got Lucas on the stretcher and rushed out of the arena through the rider's gate. Rusty's feet were like lead as he saw them take him straight to the medical area. He needed to be there. He had to find out how hurt Lucas was. *God, please. I'll do whatever you want. I'll walk away from him if that's what is needed, but I'm begging you. Make sure he's okay.*

He slowly walked back toward the medical tent area. Dread filled him.

He stopped at the tent opening, peeking inside to see Doc Milburn and his assistant working on Lucas. They looked into his eyes before shaking their heads.

Rusty needed to know what was going on. He had to know, even if it was the bad news. Bull riders were hurt on the circuit all the time. Most were not fatal injuries, but they did happen all too often.

"Doc?" he whispered as he stepped into the curtained area.

"Rusty, you shouldn't be here."

"I need to know, Doc. Is he going to be okay?"

"Right now, I don't know. He's unconscious and the longer he's that way, the worse the outcome usually."

"Can I see him?"

Doc nodded. "For a minute, then we need to get him to the hospital for tests."

Rusty walked slowly up to the side of the gurney. Lucas's eyes were already bruising around the eye sockets. He knew this wasn't a good sign.

He bent down and touched his lips to Lucas's ear. "I know you can hear me so just know that when you get better, we are going to do this right. No more stalling." A tear slipped down his cheek. "Don't leave me. I need you, Lucas. You are my heart and soul."

An ambulance crew came rushing in and took over the job of getting Lucas on the gurney and out of the arena.

"Where are you taking him?"

"St. Vincent."

"I'll be there as soon as I can. Can you tell him that if he wakes up?"

"Sure, buddy."

Rusty wanted to go to the hospital, but he knew Lucas would be mad if he didn't ride and win this event. Lucas was always put bull riding above anything else. "For you, buddy. I will win this and then I'll be by your side, no matter what."

They rushed out with Lucas tied to the gurney.

Rusty would remember that ugly scene for the rest of his life.

Chapter Fifteen

"Now up, is our comeback kid, Rusty Arnold. Rusty is holding steady in third place with his ride being the last for the night. If he covers his bull, he'll win the event hands down."

Rusty climbed up on the metal rung before sliding his leg over so he could stand spread eagle above the bull. He had to get his head on straight or he'd been in the hospital right alongside Lucas. He closed his eyes, taking a deep breath to calm his nerves. When he lowered himself on the bull's back, the animal shifted so his side was against the fence, trapping Rusty's leg against the railing. The spotter put his foot on the bull's side to push him over, releasing Rusty's leg. *That fucking hurt!*

As soon as his rope was pulled tight, he did his wrap, pounded on his fist to help close his grip on the rope, and then nodded his head.

The bull shot out, kicking and spinning to the right. With each buck, Rusty re-centered himself, riding like his life depended on it until the buzzer sounded. He'd made his eight. He could go to the hospital now.

"He did it! Rusty Arnold has won the event with that spectacular ride of ninety two points."

His best ride ever, but it didn't mean shit, not when his life lay in a hospital bed across town. He had to do his duty and accept the belt buckle, boots, and check before he could leave.

Everyone slapped him on the back, congratulating him on his great win. He smiled and said thanks, going through the motions so he could get the hell out of there.

The lights flashed as he stepped up on the shark tank to accept his winnings. The crowd chanted his name over and over.

It was a great moment, one he could thank his lucky stars for, but it didn't mean anything without Lucas by his side.

After the ceremony was over, he headed for the locker room to grab their bags, only to be stopped by Mr. Coleman.

"I'm very proud of you, Rusty. You did a fantastic job during this event. You went three for three."

"Thank you." Rusty looked over his shoulder wishing he could escape.

"I'm sure you'll do great this entire season. I'm counting on you doing well. Keep your head on your shoulders, son, and you'll come out on top."

"I appreciate it, Mr. Coleman, but I need to get going."

Mr. Coleman put his hand on Rusty's shoulder. "I saw Lucas's crash. Is he okay?"

"I don't know. He's at the hospital."

"Go then."

Rusty nodded before he turned on his heels and practically ran out to the curb to grab a cab. He let out a high pitched whistle to stop the first one going by. When he hopped into the back, he told them St. Vincent's hospital as fast as they could go.

The cab weaved in and out of traffic, but Rusty didn't care. He kept his eyes glued to the street as the streetlights went in a rapid sequence past his window. As they reached the hospital entrance, Rusty threw money at the driver and leapt out of the cab. He rushed inside, sliding to a halt at the receptionist window.

"Lucas Jacks. Where is he?"

"One moment please." She turned to her computer, tapping on the keys for several moments while he chewed on his lips in frustration. "He's still in the emergency room, sir. You'll have to take a seat."

"I need to see him."

"Are you family?"

"Yes. I'm his brother." Rusty knew the lie would bite him in the ass in the end, but he didn't care. The need to see Lucas brought out the worst in him. He had to find out if he was okay.

"Let me call into the back, and I'll see what I can do."

Rusty paced the room with his hands stuffed in his pockets. He hadn't even removed his chaps after his ride, just grabbed their bags and took off for the hospital. He could probably text Levi and have him come by to retrieve their stuff, but right now he had more important things on his mind.

"Wait right here, sir. Someone will be out to talk to you in a minute."

"Thank you."

Within a few moments, a guy in dark blue scrubs came through the door. "Who is here with Lucas Jacks?"

"I am."

"The receptionist said you were family?"

"Yes, well, sort of."

The guy's eyebrow went up. "Sort of how?"

"We are engaged."

"I see." The man looked at him with a doubtful expression on his face, but he nodded for him to follow anyway. They walked down a long, narrow hallway surrounded by room after room with gurneys and people everywhere. "Mr. Jacks has a severe concussion. His nose is broken as well as the sockets around his eyes. He won't be doing any riding for a while."

Rusty snorted knowing it would take a lot to keep Lucas from riding.

"I will be keeping him for a couple of days to monitor his head injury. He's conscious now, which is a good thing. He probably won't remember what happened and may not remember anything for a day or two before today. That's common with this type of injury." The doctor stopped at a curtained off area to his right. "You can see him, but don't stay long. The nurses will be moving him to a room pretty soon."

Rusty walked through the curtain and moved to Lucas's bedside. The monitor over his head showed his heartbeat running at a regular rhythm. It was reassuring in the most simplistic way he could think of. When he touched Lucas's hand, Lucas turned his face toward him. "Lucas?"

"Hey."

"How are you doing, buddy?"

"I feel like I've been hit by a truck. I can barely see you."

"I'm sure you can probably only see a little. Both of your eyes are almost swollen shut."

"What happened?"

"You took a shot to the face."

"Shit."

"Yeah."

"Uh, Rusty?"

"Yeah?"

"Where are we? I don't remember."

"New York, buddy. First ride of the season."

"How'd you do?"

"I won."

"That's fantastic. I knew you could do it."

"You should rest."

"I know."

"I should go."

"No, stay here with me. I don't want to be by myself."

"I can't stay the night with you, I don't think."

"Okay. Stay until they put me somewhere rather than wherever here is at the moment."

"You're in the emergency room right now. They should be moving you to a room soon."

"All right. Stay until they move me to a room then. I need you with me."

"I'll stay as long as they let me."

Lucas sighed as he relaxed into the bed when Rusty took the chair next to him. "I love you."

"I love you too, Lucas. After you get better, we need to talk though."

"Talk?"

"Yeah."

"That doesn't sound good."

"It's good. Don't worry."

"As long as you're still with me, I can handle anything."

"I'll always be with you."

Lucas's breathing evened out and Rusty could tell he slept. Healing was top priority for Lucas. If that meant they took some time off the circuit for Lucas to heal, then so be it. His life was beside this man, no matter what it took.

* * * *

Two days later, Lucas was released from the hospital. The bruises on his face had begun to fade to greenish, signaling the healing process had begun. He wouldn't be able to ride for several weeks, until the bones in his face healed, but he could be in the stands for Rusty.

The next stop on their tour wasn't too far from home. Oklahoma City.

As they drove home from New York, Rusty sat in the driver's seat whistling along with the tune on the radio. They had to rent a car in New York to get home since it wasn't a good idea for Lucas to fly with his injuries. Lucas felt itchy, like he'd forgotten something that needed to be done. His memory of the days before the accident were blurry and jumbled. His body still hurt from his tumble, but his cock worked fine and Rusty had kept them apart quoting healing time that the doctor insisted on.

He needed to come before his head exploded and his balls shriveled up and died. "Where are we stopping tonight?"

"Uh, I figured we could stop somewhere in Illinois to sleep tonight, get up early and make it home by tomorrow evening. It's about twenty hours from Chicago to Albuquerque."

"Okay." Silence stretched his nerves thin. He hated the strained tenseness between them. It wasn't like them to not be able to say whatever they felt, but Lucas wasn't sure about anything these days. Rusty hadn't said he loved him in several days, and it hurt. He wanted to curl up next to his lover, lose himself in his body, and love the night away. "Rusty?"

"Yeah?"

"Are we okay?"

"What do you mean?"

"Us. Are things okay between us?"

"Yeah, why do you ask?"

"Because you haven't touched me, kissed me, or said you loved me in days."

Rusty exhaled on a rush. "I've been holding myself at bay for you. I don't want to hurt you."

"For me?"

"Yeah. Your health is more important than my libido."

Relief went through him like being hit by lightning. Rusty was concerned about him. He'd been keeping to himself because he didn't want to hurt him. Lucas smiled and then laughed a little.

"What's so funny?"

"You."

"Me?"

"Yeah, you've been staying away from me because you care about me and all I wanted was for you to kiss me and tell me you loved me."

"I do love you, more than anything in the world."

"Thank God. I thought maybe something had changed and you figured out you didn't really love me and were trying to protect my feelings."

Rusty pulled the car to the side of the road and flipped on the hazard lights. When he reached for him, Lucas went into his arms willingly as he waited for the touch of Rusty's mouth. He didn't have to wait long as Rusty brushed his lips against Lucas's in a soft caress.

"I love you. I'm sorry if you thought something had changed to make me rethink those feelings."

"You said we had to talk when we were in the emergency room."

"Talk, yes, break up, no."

"Thank God."

"I wanted it to be somewhere special, you know, but I guess here is as good as any place." He touched Lucas on the cheek. "I love you with all my heart, and I want us to get married."

"Can we? Get married, I mean?"

"Yes. It's perfectly legal in New Mexico. I've done some research on it and gays have the right to marry in our state."

"When?"

"I don't know. We can talk about it when we get home, but does that mean yes?"

"Yes, of course, yes. I love you."

Rusty kissed him again, more forcibly this time, thrusting his tongue inside his mouth to tangle with his own. He returned the kiss stroke for stroke until they were both breathless and his cock was as hard as a rock.

"We are making love tonight. I can't wait until we get home," Lucas insisted.

"Are you sure?"

"Yeah. I need you."

"Good, because I've been dying here."

"It's a date then."

Rusty moved back to the driver's side, put the truck in gear, and merged back into traffic. "We'll stop early. I need to be inside you."

"Sounds good to me and, Rusty?"

"Yeah?"

"Hurry, would you?"

"You bet!"

Epilogue

Halfway through the riding season, and here he stood at the courthouse with his knees knocking, his palms sweaty, and his stomach in knots.

He and Lucas had decided since they had a two week break in the mid-season, they would get married. They didn't want a big ceremony, just the two of them and the justice of the peace. Nice, quiet, and low-key.

Since the season started, Lucas had lived at his house while he healed from his injuries. They'd loved the nights away, worked side-by-side on his place, and made their lives as domesticated as they could. They'd sold Lucas's house in town and invested that money in Double L Bucking Bulls. They were now partners with Logan.

He'd been by Lucas's side when they told his parents and siblings about their relationship. His father had thrown them out, his mother had taken to her room in a fit of hysteria, his sister shrugged and said whatever, and his brother had called them every foul name for a gay person he could think of. As far as Lucas was concerned, his sister was his only family.

Rusty had made peace with his father, although he didn't like what his son was, he no longer had nasty things to say to them. His mother was a saint in her acceptance of their lifestyle. Russell avoided him, and John, Thomas, and Junior had accepted Lucas with no qualms.

A glance at the clock on the wall revealed Lucas was late. Rusty felt like he was going to puke. *What if Lucas got cold feet and didn't come?* He hadn't said a word last night when they'd split up, preferring not to see each other before the ceremony.

"Son? Is your partner coming?" the clerk asked as she pulled her glasses down on her nose so she could look over the top of them at him.

"I, uh…I'm not sure."

There was a ruckus out in the front hall. Several voices could be heard shouting.

Rusty looked at the clerk and then looked back at the door.

A moment later, the double doors burst open and a wave of people came into the room, Lucas at the front of the crowd. The big grin on his face gave away his excitement.

"Lucas? What's going on?"

"I know you wanted to make this simple with only a couple of people here, but I wanted to share this day with those who support us."

Rusty looked over the crowd, recognizing several faces from the circuit including Levi and Curt, C.B. Parker, Jefferson Thompson, Butch Reardon, his mother, John, Thomas, and Junior, Lucas's sister Sheryl, as well as a few he knew only a little. "Wow."

Levi came forward and hugged him. "We wanted to celebrate this special day with you and Lucas. When Lucas called, we all hopped in our vehicles and came out to be with you two as you said your vows. I hope you have room at your place to put us up."

Levi grinned as Rusty laughed. "I'm sure I can find room. There's always the hay loft."

"Can we get this show on the road, please? I have another ceremony in a few minutes." The judge signaled for them to come toward him.

"Sorry."

Lucas took his hand as they walked toward the judge. The crowd circled behind them, closing them in a cocoon of acceptance.

As the judge went through the normal ceremonial words and they got to the exchanging vows part, Rusty turned to look at Lucas. Tears sparkled on Lucas's eyelashes as he repeated the vows that would bind them together for the rest of their lives in the eyes of God and the state of New Mexico. When it came to his turn to say his vows, he almost couldn't speak. His throat was constricted with emotion so strong, he'd bet his life that he would remember the look on Lucas's face until the day he died.

"I love you," Rusty whispered as he slipped the gold band onto Lucas's finger.

"I love you."

"You may now kiss your spouse."

Rusty leaned in, bringing his mouth to within a hairsbreadth away from Lucas's before he grinned and locked their mouths together in a soul-melting kiss.

"Ladies and gentleman. May I present Mr. Rusty Arnold and his husband, Mr. Lucas Jacks. May your union be blessed with children, long and loving days, and a bright and shiny future."

Rusty pulled Lucas into a hug before they turned to face their friends.

"Let's party!"

The End

About the Author

Sandy Sullivan is a romance author, who, when not writing, spends her time with her husband Shaun on their farm in middle Tennessee. She loves to ride her horses, play with their dogs and relax on the porch, enjoying the rolling hills of her home south of Nashville. Country music is a passion of hers and she loves to listen to it while she writes.

She is an avid reader of romance novels and enjoys reading Nora Roberts, Jude Deveraux and Susan Wiggs. Finding new authors and delving into something different helps feed the need for literature. A registered nurse by education, she loves to help people and spread the enjoyment of romance to those around her with her novels. She loves cowboys so you'll find many of her novels have sexy men in tight jeans and cowboy boots.

Sandy's website
www.romancestorytime.com

Other books by Sandy

Love Me Once, Love Me Twice (Montana Cowboys 1)
Before the Night is Over (Montana Cowboys 2)
Two for the Price of One (Montana Cowboys 3)
Difficult Choices (Montana Cowboys 4)
Doctor Me Up (Montana Cowboys 5)
Stakin' His Claim
Country Minded Cougar

Meet Me in the Barn
Taming the Cougar
Trouble With a Cowboy
Gotta Love a Cowboy
Make Mine a Cowboy (Cowboy Dreamin' 1)
Healing a Cowboy's Heart (Cowboy Dreamin' 2)
For the Love of a Cowboy (Cowboy Dreamin' 3)
Tempted by the Cowboy (Cowboy Dreamin' 4)
Forever Kind of Cowboy (Cowboy Dreamin' 5)
Kiss Me, Cowboy (Cowboy Dreamin' 6)
A Cowboy and a Country Song (Cowboy Dreamin' 7)
Loving Hard (Eight Second Ride Book 1)